Corpse in the Cactus
(A Sunshine Valley Mystery)

by

Rita Strombeck

For information, email **Cozy Cat Press**, cozycatpress@aol.com or visit our website at: www.cozycatpress.com

COZY CAT
P R E S S

ISBN: 978-1-939816-57-3

Printed in the United States of America

Cover design by Karri Klawiter
http://artbykarri.com/cover-art/e-book-print-cover-art-design/

1 2 3 4 5 6 7 8 9 10

For Dolores Nicholas, a very supportive friend

Chapter 1

"I can't believe what I'm seeing," said Eve Iverson, as she followed her husband Adam to the hostess who was standing behind a tall counter. Looking around the large restaurant, she made a sweeping gesture with her hand. "All these paintings hanging on the walls and my cactus is one of them . . . and the one that was stolen from the gallery, at that. I sure would like to find out how it got here."

"Don't worry," replied Adam, as he glanced over at his wife's canvas that was hanging on a side wall. "We can ask the hostess. I'm sure somebody in here has an answer."

Lunch is generally the busiest time of the day in the Crazy Cactus and today was no different. Voices, high and low, filled the air and servers who were wearing colorful shirts and carrying loaded trays from the kitchen, placed dishes filled with an assortment of Mexican entrées on the blue and white tiled tables.

Adam had to stand behind a short line of customers before he was able to reach the hostess. When she finished writing down the name of the last customer, he explained about his wife's stolen painting and asked if he could speak to the manager or someone else who might have some knowledge about it. He pointed to Eve's canvas, but the woman just looked at him blankly and shrugged her shoulders. She was cordial, but somewhat aloof. "I have no idea how, or when, it got here. As you can see," she said, waving her arm around the room, "we have so many paintings." After a slight pause, she continued. "I think you'll have to speak to Mr. Wolf about this matter. He's the owner and handles all the paintings. He's the only person who may be able to help you. I'll have someone show you back to his office. It's too crowded and noisy out here to talk."

The hostess walked over to another woman who was standing a few feet behind her and whispered some words in her ear. After a few seconds, the two women approached Adam and Eve. "This is Maria, my assistant. She'll show you to Mr. Wolf's office. I'm sure he'll be able to answer any questions you might have."

"Follow me," said Maria, a short woman with curly dark hair. "We have to go to the back," she added, with a smile, then turned and began walking towards the rear of the restaurant.

As Adam and Eve began to follow the woman, several customers who were waiting for a table glared at them. Ignoring the looks, the Iversons slowly made their way through the crowded aisle, careful not to bump into anyone.

"Boy, I can't wait to eat here," said Eve. "Everything looks and smells so wonderful. I'm going to have the chile rellenos and guacamole . . . I think that's what they're having," she commented, as she passed a man and woman who were sitting at a table. "The food looks scrumptious. There must be almost a hundred people in here who think so too. Let's get this question answered as soon as possible, so we can enjoy our lunch."

"You don't seem very upset about your painting," remarked Adam.

"I can't say that I am. I know it's wrong to steal, but I'm happy to see that my painting is hanging in such a beautiful place. Somebody must have really liked it. I'm just curious to find out who wanted it badly enough to steal it. This place is a veritable art gallery. I wonder if mine is the only one that was stolen."

When they reached the back of the restaurant, Maria stopped. "Mr. Wolf's office is right this way," she said, pointing to an open doorway that led down a long, dark hall. "I'm sure he'll be able to tell you what you want to know."

With Maria in the lead, Adam and Eve followed closely behind. As they approached the office, the door swung open and a tall man, wearing a large brimmed hat, emerged. As soon as he saw the three of them coming towards him, he turned abruptly and ran the other way, then made a quick exit through a rear door.

"What was that all about?" asked Eve.

"That was George Gomez. He used to work in the restaurant. I don't know what he's doing here now and I don't understand why he ran away when he saw us," Maria replied, seemingly puzzled.

As they were getting ready to enter the office, Eve remarked, "There certainly are a lot of instructions on this door. Look here," she said as she read each one:

"Dick Wolf, Proprietor and Manager"
"Knock Before Entering"
"No Loitering"
"No Soliciting"

"Mr. Wolf usually doesn't like to be disturbed when he's working," Maria explained, meekly.

"Well," said Adam, "the door is slightly open. Let's just knock and see if he hears us."

Following his suggestion, Maria tapped lightly on the door, but no one answered. She repeated her knock, this time a little louder, but still no answer. "Mr. Wolf?" she called, tentatively, as she slowly opened the door with difficulty, pushing aside a large book that was lying on the floor and blocking the entrance. Once she stepped into the office, she let out a loud gasp, and then jumped back. "He's on the floor," she exclaimed. "It's Mr. Wolf and he's lying on the floor."

Adam rushed into the room and over to the body of a large man in a soiled white shirt who was lying sideways in what appeared to be a small pool of blood. "I don't feel a pulse," he said, as he bent down and held the man's wrist. "I think he may have been shot and there's something that looks like a letter opener in his right hand."

After a few seconds, Adam stood up and walked over to Eve and Maria. They both stood back, staring wide-eyed at the body on the floor. "Be careful not to touch anything," he cautioned. "Maria, there must be a phone in the dining room. We need to report this. Can you go and call the sheriff?"

"Yes, yes, of course. I'll do it right away," she said, as she turned to leave the room. "Wait," continued Adam, "He's probably going to ask us to lock all the doors until he and his men get here. Do you know if there's a key for the one in the rear where George Gomez ran out? I think we need to lock it too."

"Yes," replied Maria, as she reached into her pocket. "We all have one. Here, take this," she said and handed a key on a chain to Adam. She turned and left the room, once again with difficulty, as she pushed against the book on the floor.

"I'll go and lock the back door," said Adam. "In the meantime, Eve, you stand outside in the hall and guard the office. Whatever you do, don't let anyone enter."

"Yes, sir," replied Eve, then she and her husband quickly exited the office.

It didn't take long before both Adam and Maria returned to the scene.

"I called the sheriff," gasped Maria. "He said he was sending help right away and would be here shortly, himself. You were right, Adam. He said to lock all the doors and not let anyone in or out until his men arrive. One of the staff is doing that now. He also said not to touch anything. I'm afraid it's going to be a madhouse out there, when people discover they're not allowed to leave, and that the owner's been shot. I hope the sheriff gets here soon."

Following closely behind Maria were two men, one of whom was carrying a large tray with several dishes of food on it. They were intent upon entering the office, but were immediately blocked by Adam. "You can't go in there. I'm afraid Mr. Wolf won't be having lunch today. A crime may have been committed and, if so, you need to stay out, or you could be accused of tampering with evidence." His tone was serious, as he spoke to the men. They instantly obeyed and backed away.

"Good," continued Adam. "Now, why don't all of you go back into the dining room and wait for the sheriff and his men. Maria, you can escort him and his team back here when they arrive. I'll continue to guard the door." As requested, they all followed Adam's suggestions.

"Well, here we go," said Eve, as she took Maria's arm. "I'm sure the news has already spread, but, I hope it's not too chaotic out there."

The two women walked slowly, fearing what they were about to encounter. However, once they re-entered the large dining area, Eve was astounded by what she saw and heard. Contrary to her expectations, most diners were still seated at their tables and continued enjoying their meals, as usual. Nobody seemed the least bit upset. As for the employees, however, the situation was just the opposite. Waiters and waitresses, alike, were shouting and laughing. "The big, bad wolf is dead . . . I killed the beast . . . The beast is dead . . . No, I killed him . . . No, I killed the wolf." One after another, both men and women were claiming responsibility for killing Dick Wolf.

"My goodness," remarked Eve. "This certainly is not what I anticipated. I've never seen anything like this. Usually, if someone has been murdered, people who were close to the victim want to claim their innocence, not their guilt. On the surface, this is such a lovely restaurant, but I have a feeling things are very different behind the scenes. Everyone who works here appears to want to claim responsibility for killing the owner. Crazy Cactus certainly seems like an appropriate name for this restaurant."

"I have to tell you," said Maria, grinning broadly, "Mr. Wolf isn't, I mean, he wasn't, an easy person to work for. Now that he's dead, I can say this. He fired quite a few of the staff when he took over, like George Gomez, and he threatened many others. I even heard him once say that he wouldn't stop at killing an employee, if that was the only way to get rid of him or her. As you can see, I think everyone who works here is thrilled at the news. I was quite shaken when I first saw the body, but I can't say it makes me sad that he's dead. He was a very mean man and made many enemies."

The shouting and bragging continued. Every once in a while, a few diners would look up and laugh. *They probably think this is part of the entertainment,* thought Eve. Only a few people attempted to leave, but, when the hostess said something to them, they seated themselves, without protest, in the waiting area.

Eve walked over to the front window and, after a few minutes, noticed the arrival of the sheriff and his team. From all she could see, they tried to avoid blocking legally parked cars. The hostess went to unlock the front door and a line of six law enforcement officers, including Sheriff Bud Warner, entered the restaurant. She then turned and began leading the group to the back office.

When Sheriff Warner spotted Eve, he stopped abruptly. "Well," he said, with a wry grin, "It's you again. I can't say I'm surprised. When I was told that a husband and his wife had discovered a dead body, I should have known it was the Iversons who found the corpse in the cactus. The discovery of dead bodies is becoming quite a habit with you two."

"I certainly hope not," replied Eve. She began to offer an explanation for their presence in the restaurant, but Sheriff Warner held up his hand. "Don't say a word. We'll get your statement later. Just show me where to go." Eve obeyed and led him to the scene of the crime.

As she began walking towards the rear of the restaurant, Eve noticed two officers standing by the kitchen entrance. One of them began speaking in a loud, but calm, voice. "Quiet please. May I have everyone's attention?" He was addressing the diners. A sudden hush fell over the room. "You are to remain seated at your tables until one of the officers has spoken with you. No one is to leave until then. There's nothing to worry about. Just keep calm and remain seated."

By now, most of the diners realized that this was not entertainment and stopped eating. A look of bewilderment appeared on most faces, but no one made any attempt to get up and leave. Eve heard some screaming coming from the kitchen area. A number of employees were still yelling, claiming they killed the owner. The remaining staff stood quietly in a corner in the main dining room, waiting to see what would happen next.

When Eve and the sheriff arrived at the back office, Adam was standing in the hallway. The door was wide open. Two officers were on their knees and appeared to be examining the body on the floor.

Sheriff Warner approached Adam and began to speak. "Well, as I was telling your wife, I should have suspected you two were somehow involved in this caper. I know you were made honorary deputy sheriffs, but perhaps we need to hire you for real."

"No, thank you," replied Adam. "We're not looking for a job."

"In any case, we're going to need your statements. Why don't you and Eve go over to Sergeant Spaulding? You can tell him everything you saw and heard." The sheriff pointed to an officer standing a few feet down the hallway. "In the meantime, I'll see what forensics has to say," he added, then turned and entered the office.

Adam and Eve did as they were directed and, after describing everything they'd witnessed, including the stolen painting and the encounter with George Gomez, they were told they could leave, but to be prepared to come to the station, if there were more questions.

"That's a relief," sighed Eve. "I've had enough. Let's go," she said to Adam, then took his hand. "The sooner we get out of here, the better. I don't want to see or hear anything else."

As the couple headed for the front door, they noticed that more than half of the tables in the dining room were now empty. "Sheriff Warner is sure going to have his hands full with the staff," said Eve. "I've never seen so many people claim they killed a person. It's almost as if they were standing in line, waiting to admit their guilt. I know they weren't serious, but maybe one. . . or more . . .actually did kill Dick Wolf. Apparently, he wasn't very well liked. By the way," she continued, "I thought he was Deputy Sheriff Warner and yet, I heard everyone, including you, call him Sheriff."

"I think I forgot to tell you. He was promoted after Olive's case," Adam explained.

"Olive?"

"You know . . .Olive Howell? Our neighbor Frank's wife? The dead woman we found in the hot tub? Did you forget so soon?" Adam chided.

"Yes. Of course. I certainly haven't forgotten. I was just wondering why he received a promotion, since you and I pretty much solved the case for him."

"Well, that's the way it goes here," sighed Adam. "He became a full-fledged sheriff and we were made honorary deputies."

"I hate to say this, but, he didn't appear to be particularly upset by the fact that a murder may have been committed here. He even made a joke. In fact, nobody seems very upset . . .just the opposite."

For the last time, Eve looked over at her painting and sighed. "I wish we'd never seen my stolen canvas. I just wanted to find out how it got here and, because of that, we're now embroiled in a real mess. But, you really handled everything very well. You knew exactly what to do and what not to do and you've remained so calm. I'm very proud of you."

"Thank you, honorary deputy. You know that I watch a lot of crime shows on television and I've learned quite a bit over the years. I just didn't think my knowledge would come in so handy in real life."

As they approached the front of the restaurant, they were stopped by a uniformed officer. Adam explained that they'd given their statements to Sergeant Spaulding, who'd told them they were now free to go. Seemingly satisfied, the officer opened the door for the couple and allowed them to leave.

"I want to get out of here before the press gets wind of this," said Eve, as she rushed outside. "I'm sure the place will soon be swarming with reporters and I don't want any pictures taken or have to give any interviews."

When they reached their car, Eve plopped herself down in the passenger seat and let out a deep sigh. "This is crazy," she gasped. "For a second, I thought my watch had stopped. We've only been here a little over an hour. It seems like it's been much longer and we haven't even eaten yet. I'm still hungry, aren't you?"

"Yes, I am. Should we look for another restaurant? There are quite a few good ones in town. Some of them even serve Mexican food. I think we might be able to find one that doesn't have a dead body in it."

"No. . . please . . . With our luck, I'm afraid of what we might encounter. For now, let's just go home and dig something out of the refrigerator."

"Whatever you wish," replied Adam, as he started to drive and passed an ambulance that was just pulling into the restaurant's service entrance.

"You know," remarked Eve, "I thought everything was supposed to be tranquil here in paradise. So far, it's been just the opposite."

"Well," replied Adam, "don't forget, this is still the wild west. I think we're bound to run into some leftovers from its turbulent past."

"I hope you're wrong. I just want some peace . . .no turbulence, thank you."

The trip home was quiet and neither Adam, nor Eve, wished to speak about any of the events they'd just experienced. Pulling into their driveway, they heard Coco barking and they both began to laugh.

"You know," said Adam, "they say that dogs have an excellent sense of both smell and hearing."

"Well," replied Eve, "I hope Coco heard us and didn't smell us. After what we've just been through, I'm afraid I'm a bit stinky."

Upon entering the house, both Adam and Eve were accosted by their poodle, who began jumping up and running in circles around both of them.

"Hi there, little girl, we haven't been gone that long and we're happy to see you too," said Adam, as he leaned over and petted the dog.

"We sure are," sighed Eve, as she also bent down to stroke Coco's black, curly head. "I'm glad we decided to come back home. This is so much nicer, compared to the place we just left."

Chapter 2

As Eve started to go into the kitchen to see if she could find something suitable for lunch, the doorbell rang. "Oh, no," she sighed. "Now, who can that be? I hope there's no more trouble."

"I'll get it," said Adam. When he opened the front door, he was met by one of their neighbors, Doty O'Brien. "I'm so glad you're back home. We saw you pull up. We're over at Frank's house and having a barbecue. We got a late start. Have you two eaten yet? If not, do you think you could come over? We'd love it if you could join us."

"Hi, Doty," said Eve, as she approached the two of them. "Actually, your timing is perfect. I was just on my way into the kitchen to fix some lunch when you rang the bell. We'd love to join you, but are you sure there's enough food for two more hungry people?"

"Yes . . . and then some. We made a huge barbecue. We're having ribs, chicken tacos al carbon, corn on the cob, and guacamole. I hope you like Mexican food."

"Absolutely. That's what we were going to have today, but our plans got changed," replied Eve. "Is it okay if we bring Coco with us?"

"You know you never need to ask. Of course, Coco is welcome," replied Doty.

"Okay. Just let me change my blouse and we'll be right over."

"Great . . . and I want you to meet our friend Jackie. She's new here, but, I've known her ever since we were little. You'll love her. Come on over when you're ready."

"I hope this is okay with you," said Eve, as she closed the door and looked at Adam.

"Not a problem, my dear. I'm quite happy to go to a barbecue at Frank's place. The food is always very good and we won't have to cook. I think it will be fun."

Eve turned and went into the bedroom and returned to the living room a few minutes later, after putting on a clean blouse. "I'm ready now and starving. Let's go."

Adam adjusted Coco's leash and the three of them exited through the patio, taking a quick route across the gravel path to their neighbor's house. Once they entered his patio and closed the gate, everyone began welcoming the trio. Besides Frank, they were greeted by the Irish sisters, Doty and Paula, and another woman they didn't recognize.

"Come on in," said Paula, as she rose unsteadily to her feet. "We're so happy you could join us. I want you to meet someone very special," she added, as she led the tall dark-haired woman forward and introduced her to the new arrivals.

"Hello . . . and hello to you too," said the woman, as she reached down to pet Coco, who was scampering around the patio, eager to greet everyone. "I'm Jaqueline Quinn, but you can call me Jackie . . . everybody else does. When I was little, some of the kids used to tease me, claiming that Jackie was a boy's name, but I don't have any such problems now," she said, with a laugh.

"We've known Jackie ever since the last century," Doty began to explain. "She and Paula and I all went to the same grammar school in Milwaukee and we've been friends ever since. But, I never heard anyone tease you like that," she added, as she looked at her friend.

"That happened at the first school I attended. I was so glad when my parents moved and enrolled me in a new school. That's how I met you and Paula," continued Jackie. "If they hadn't moved, I wouldn't be sitting here now."

"So nice to meet you," said Eve, as she and Adam both reached out and shook the woman's hand. "I'd say that was a good move. Are you Irish too? We have the two Irish sisters here . . . Doty O'Brien and Paula McGuire. I know they're not related, but that's what everyone calls them. Perhaps we now have a triplet?"

"No," laughed Paula. "Jackie's background is French, but we still accept her."

"You bet," added Doty. "When we were in grammar school, we did everything together. Paula used to call us the three musketeers . . . one for all and all for one. Now, I'm so thrilled that Jackie has moved here and the three of us are back together again."

"Quinn is my married name," Jackie began to explain. "My husband was Irish. When he passed away, I didn't want to remain in Milwaukee by myself. I have a couple of cousins who live in Mexico and they invited me to join them, but I wanted to remain in the States. Then, Doty and Paula urged me to come out here and see if I thought it was a place where I could live. Like so many others before me, I immediately fell in love with Sunshine Valley. It didn't take long to find a beautiful house and make a quick move. It's been about two months now and this is where I plan to stay."

"Well, welcome to Sunshine Valley. I'm sure you're going to enjoy living here," said Adam.

"Parlez-vous français?" asked Eve.

"Un peu," replied Jackie. "I took French in high school, but only for about two years. I think it's a beautiful language and have always wished I could speak it."

"Well," said Eve. "I used to teach French. Perhaps we can form a little French conversation circle, after you settle in."

"I'd love that." Jackie was all smiles.

"I haven't seen you at the pool. Do you swim?" asked Eve.

"I certainly do. Right now, however, I'm a little stiff," she remarked as she rubbed her shoulders. "It's from all the unpacking. I think I brought too much with me. But, trust me, once I get settled and have everything in order, you'll find me at the pool just about every day. I used to go swimming at an indoor pool in Milwaukee and I can't wait to jump into an outdoor pool."

"Great. I look forward to seeing you there. We can do laps together." Eve glanced around the patio and smiled. "What a treat this is for us," she commented. "You have no idea what we've been through today. We decided to try the Crazy Cactus for lunch, but, unfortunately, it didn't work out as planned . . . too many problems."

"You were at the Crazy Cactus? Don't tell me. By any chance, are you the couple who found the dead body of the owner?" Paula interjected.

Eve was stunned by the question. "How did you know about that? Yes, sad to say, we're the ones, but how . . ."

Paula didn't let her finish. "We just heard about it on the radio . . . news flash. The report said the owner of the Crazy Cactus was found dead in his office by a married couple . . . and a man was seen fleeing the building. No names were given. But, tell me . . . how did you happen to discover the body?"

Eve hesitated, wondering if she should offer an explanation, then thought better of it. "It was awful, but I really don't want to talk about it. Adam and I have had quite a hectic day so far and, now, I just want to enjoy myself and try to clear my mind of any unpleasant thoughts. I'll tell you all about it later, when I've had a chance to regain my composure."

"I was at the Crazy Cactus too," chirped Jackie.

"You were? I didn't see you there," responded Eve, in surprise.

"I went early . . . to avoid the crowds. I wanted to get some flan for our dessert. They make the best. So, I placed an order yesterday and went there before noon to pick it up."

"We must have just missed each other. Did you see or hear anything?" asked Eve, with some reluctance.

Jackie cheerfully continued. "No, nothing unusual. I wasn't there very long. I just waited up front, by the hostess, until someone brought my order. The only thing I saw was lots of happy diners, who were enjoying their food."

"We've been to the Crazy Cactus several times . . . the four of us . . . and never saw or heard anything out of the ordinary," explained Paula. "The food is good and the service is always excellent. I don't think we ever met the owner, but I'm really surprised to hear what happened. It must have been very upsetting to find a dead body, but I'm glad to see that you two are okay. You can tell me more some other time."

Adam was also reluctant to get involved in any conversation about the discovery of Dick Wolf's body and walked over to Frank, who was standing by the grill. "That really looks good," he said, as he placed an arm over the shoulder of his neighbor.

"I think I've made enough to feed the entire valley," replied Frank, with a laugh.

"Just wait. I'm starving and I know Eve is also very hungry. Believe me, we'll do justice to this feast. It really smells wonderful," added Adam, as he took a deep breath.

"Okay, it's time to sit down," commanded Paula, as she invited everyone to take a seat. "Wherever you like . . . it doesn't matter."

They all followed Paula's lead, except for Doty, who remained standing by the grill. "I'm going to help Frank serve," she announced, as she carried the first plate on a tray and set it down in front of Jackie. "I even have something to drink for our little furry friend," she added, as she placed a bowl under the table. Coco, who had now settled herself on the ground, next to Eve, leaned over and began lapping up the water.

"Can I give her a piece of chicken?" Jackie asked Eve. "Coco is a girl, right?"

"Yes, she sure is. Generally, I don't like to share our food, but today is kind of special. Just give her one or two small pieces. I think that should make her happy."

"Dogs are wonderful," added Jackie. "They always love their owners, no matter what they do or how they look, and they're such good companions. Maybe I'll get a dog myself, once I get settled."

Eve looked at the woman and smiled, a bit surprised that she and Doty and Paula were such good friends. Eve thought she looked quite chic in her red dress, while her two friends just sported their usual drab beige desert outfits. As for looks, there was no resemblance. Jackie wore quite a bit of makeup and had dark, curly hair, *probably dyed*, thought Eve, while Doty and Paula each sported short gray locks and wore no makeup.

After everyone was served, Doty and Frank joined the others at the table. Frank poured white wine into his glass and passed the bottle. "I'd like to welcome everyone," he said, lifting his glass. "And a very special welcome to the newest resident of Sunshine Valley . . .

here's to Jackie . . . may she grow to love our little sanctuary as much as we all do."

Following Frank's lead, everyone lifted their glasses and cheered.

"This is truly an unexpected and wonderful surprise," said Eve, as she looked at her host. "The food looks fabulous and I always love your patio," she added. "You have such beautiful bushes and flowers. They're especially lovely this time of the year."

"Thank you," replied Frank. "I love to garden and I have time now. It's nice and cool today, but I want to plant some more cactus plants over there, before the hot summer weather hits us," he added, pointing to a bare space along one of the stucco walls. "But, as for the food, I just took care of the grill. We have to thank Doty and Paula for all the prep work. They really know what they're doing, when it comes to cooking. Here's to Paula and Doty, for helping to create another fabulous feast." He raised his glass, as did Eve, Adam, and Jackie.

As the afternoon wore on, conversation around the table was nonstop and covered everything from each person's childhood up to the present. Not another word was spoken about Adam and Eve's discovery of the dead body.

At one point, Jackie looked at Eve and asked, "Have you ever been to the casino? I hear there's one just outside of Tucson. I'd love to go one day and try my luck, but, none of my friends here want to go there."

"Too risky," commented Paula. "It's a sure way to throw away your money."

"Adam and I haven't been there either," began Eve. "I'm not a big fan of gambling. Even though I love games and puzzles, for some reason, my mind tends to wander when I play a slot machine. We went to Las Vegas once and it was a good thing Adam was sitting next to me. I was playing on a machine, but not paying attention to what was happening. All of a sudden, Adam stopped me, before I could continue. Lo and behold! He informed me that I just won a thousand dollar jackpot. That was sheer luck . . . or, in my case, dumb luck. So, Jackie, I'm afraid Adam and I probably won't be going to the casino . . . sorry."

After finishing two portions of food and several glasses of wine, Eve leaned back and rubbed her stomach. "What a delicious meal. As you can tell, I enjoyed every bit. This has truly been a wonderful ending to a day that had a less than pleasant beginning. A friend of mine once told me that, sometimes, when a day starts out negatively, it can end on a positive note. That certainly has been the case today. I hate to admit it, but, after everything that has happened, and after eating and drinking so much, I'm a bit weary and feel I have to excuse myself and go home and stretch out. I hope you all don't mind, but I'm really done in."

"No, certainly," said Paula. "Go home and get some rest. After what you went through, I'm not surprised that you're tired. We will all have plenty of other fine dining experiences in the future."

"Thank you," responded Eve. Then, turning to Adam, she said, "You can stay if you like. I'm just exhausted."

"No. I have to confess, this day has hit me, as well. I'm coming with you." He and Eve thanked everyone again, then he put on Coco's leash, and the three of them headed for home.

As they made their way back across the path, crunching the gravel beneath their feet, Eve turned to Adam. "That was really lovely," she said thoughtfully. "I wish we could have stayed longer, but I'm bushed. Jackie seems very nice, so outgoing and friendly. I look forward to seeing her again."

"Yes, I'm sure she'll be fun to have as a friend," replied Adam.

"I know that she and Doty and Paula all went to grammar school together, but Jackie looks much younger . . . perhaps it's the makeup. She may even have had a little cosmetic surgery. She really looks lovely," said Eve.

"We're all about the same age . . . true baby boomers."

"I think Frank is happy she's here too," Eve continued. "He really seemed to be in good spirits, more so than I've seen him in a long time. Now, that he no longer has Olive to constantly criticize him, maybe something will develop there. Did you see the way the two of them looked at each other?"

"No, I didn't notice. I was too preoccupied with the food. But," Adam added hesitatingly, "you always seem to observe everything that's going on . . . so, you may be right."

"I'm an artist, remember? I'm visual. I like to take in everything there is to see," Eve responded, then stopped, as they reached their front door.

Once they were back in the quiet of their own surroundings, Eve let out a deep sigh. "Home at last. I'm tired, but it's a bit early to go to bed. I think I'll just try to tune out and see if there's an old movie on television that I can enjoy, but, no news. I've had enough news for one day."

She had barely finished her thought when the doorbell rang. "Oh, no," she whimpered.

"I'll get it." Adam reached down to unleash the dog who had started barking, then headed for the door. "Stay Coco . . . it's okay."

There stood Doty, smiling and holding a tray in her hands. "You forgot your flan," she said, reaching out.

"Oh, Doty. We've been a little distracted today," said Eve, as she moved closer to the woman. "How nice of you to bring this over."

"Here, I'll take it into the kitchen," said Adam, as he reached for the tray and left the room.

"Come in for a second," said Eve. "That was such a lovely barbecue. I want to thank you for inviting us."

Although she was tired, Eve sensed that Doty was eager to talk, so she led her neighbor into the living room and encouraged her to be seated.

"Let's just sit here. It's easier than standing." As each of the two women sat back in an arm chair, Eve continued speaking. "We really enjoyed meeting your friend Jackie. She's a delight . . . so cheerful and friendly."

"Yes, she is very upbeat," said Doty, as she leaned forward, "but, I have to say, you saw a different woman today than Paula and I have known all our lives." She spoke in a hushed tone, as if afraid someone might overhear what she was saying.

"What do you mean?" asked Eve, puzzled.

"When we first met Jackie . . . I think we were about nine or ten . . . she was extremely shy and withdrawn. She hardly said a word. I tried to make friends with her, because she was new at school, but nothing I did seemed to work. I almost gave up, but Paula encouraged me to keep trying. Slowly, and I mean very slowly, she began to emerge from her shell. But, I must say, Jackie was never what you would call outgoing. We remained friends over the years, but it was difficult at times. Paula and I were really surprised when she told us that she was going to get married. We met her husband once or twice. He seemed very kind and supportive. We both thought he would be good for her and we were very sorry to hear when he suddenly passed away. But, let me tell you, ever since she moved to Sunshine Valley, we've seen a different person. You would never know this was the same Jackie Quinn that we've known all these years. Now, she seems cheerful and is eager to do things and go places with us. She and Frank seem to hit it off, as well. I think today is probably the happiest I've ever seen her in the fifty-odd years we've known each other. I'm really glad she decided to move to Sunshine Valley. I think it will be good for all of us."

"Well, I've heard several people say they've never felt better since moving here," responded Eve. "I'm sure Jackie will love our little haven and I look forward to seeing her again and doing laps with her in the pool and, maybe, even get to speak a little French."

"Enough," said Doty, as she pushed herself out of the chair. "I know you're tired and that this has been a difficult day for you and Adam. You have better things to do than sit here and listen to me. I'll be going now and I hope you enjoy the flan."

"We certainly will. I guarantee it." Eve escorted her neighbor to the door. "Thanks again for everything," she said, as she hugged Doty.

After closing the door, Eve turned to Adam, who had just returned from the kitchen. "That was interesting," she said. "Sunshine Valley seems to make people very happy. You know, I was thinking about a brief comment Jackie made. Did you hear it? She said that, when she was growing up, other children teased her about her name. I remember a time when I was in grammar school and was also teased. I think it was in third or fourth grade. The boy who sat behind me used to poke me in the back and call me "smarty pants," whenever I would raise my hand to answer the teacher's question. She finally noticed it and changed his seat. That was the end of it, thank goodness. It was really annoying. It's funny how, from time to time, we remember certain things from our childhood. Did anyone ever pick on you when you were little?"

"No. If they had, I would have hit them," replied Adam.

"That's what boys do. Girls don't usually get into fist fights," replied Eve. After a brief pause, she took a deep breath. "Now, finally, I intend to relax," she sighed. "I'm going to see if I can find a movie, or maybe even some game shows . . . I just want to tune out and I don't want to hear anything bad."

"Would you like some flan?" asked Adam.

"Uhuh . . . tomorrow maybe. I don't think I could eat anything more today . . . I'm really full," Eve responded, as she rubbed her stomach.

"As you wish, my dear. I'll just take Coco for a short walk, then I'll join you." He put on the dog's leash and made a quick exit. Eve turned and slowly walked into the den, then threw herself onto the couch.

Chapter 3

Just as she feared, Eve had a very restless night. She couldn't help rehashing everything that had happened during the day. Although she tried to get it out of her mind, she kept seeing the body of Dick Wolf lying on the floor. After tossing and turning in bed for several hours, she finally fell asleep some time near midnight. Upon awakening, she rubbed her eyes and looked around the room. The curtains were drawn open and the morning sun came pouring into the room, but, neither Adam, nor Coco, were anywhere to be seen. She threw back the covers, raised herself slowly, and then stumbled into the kitchen. *A strong cup of coffee is what I need now*, she thought.

It didn't take long for Adam to join her. "Well, I see you finally made it," he said, consolingly. "I thought you might have some trouble sleeping, after the events of yesterday. How do you feel?"

"A little groggy, but otherwise okay. Of course, I went over all the events of the day. Then, when I finally managed to put those thoughts aside, I began to have all sorts of weird hallucinations. I saw a lot of strange people coming and going. I didn't recognize anyone. I felt as if I had wandered into someone else's dream."

"Well, I'm sure today will be a little calmer," said Adam, reassuringly.

"I certainly hope so. I would hate to repeat the events of yesterday. But, look at you," continued Eve, "you're all dressed. I get the impression that you're going somewhere."

"Yes. I'm just on my way out. I was hoping you'd be up before I left. Sheriff Warner called a little while ago. Based on the statements we gave yesterday, he has some more questions, but he said only one of us needs to come down to the station. So, that's where I'm headed now."

"Oh, dear. I thought we were finished with that mess. Please let it be a short interview," Eve remarked, as if speaking to herself, then took a sip of her coffee.

"Maybe you should go back to bed and get some more rest," said Adam.

"No," replied Eve. "I think I'm going to do some painting this morning. It really relaxes me and helps me shut out the real world. That's what I feel I need most right now."

"Good idea. I don't know how long this will take, but I'll come directly home, as soon as we're finished," Adam assured his wife, then turned, blew her a kiss, and left the house.

After finishing her coffee, Eve returned to the bedroom, took a shower, and dressed for the day. She filled a can with water for her paint brushes, then walked out onto the patio, or, as she liked to call it, her studio. Across the way, she noticed their neighbor Frank, who appeared to be doing some gardening. Sitting down in front of her easel, with Coco by her feet, she began thumbing through some rough sketches that she'd made a few days earlier, then opted for a mountain scene.

Eve had always admired the works of Georgia O'Keeffe. When she first began painting, she'd used her for inspiration, especially her large bright, close-up blossoms. *It was almost like looking through a magnifying glass,* she thought. However, after attending an exhibit of Southwestern artists in Scottsdale, she became a fan of Fritz Scholder. She admired his loose technique. His paintings weren't as tightly rendered as O'Keefe's. She loved his scenes of the desert and the unusual way he applied colors. Now, he was the artist she kept in mind as she created her desert landscapes.

No sooner had Eve started drawing, when Coco sprang up and began barking. "Relax, Coco," she said, but the dog continued barking and ran back into the house through her own personal doggie door. *I better see what's bothering her,* she thought. *Maybe something fell down.* But, as Eve rose and went back into the house, she saw Coco run to the front door. This was followed by some quiet, but steady knocking.

Upon opening the door, Eve was confronted by a man wearing a large brimmed hat. She immediately recognized George Gomez, the man she and Adam had seen running out of Dick Wolf's office. He was looking directly at her. Suddenly, her heart started pounding.

Eve must have appeared frightened to the man, who now removed his hat and began to speak. "Hello, Mrs. Iverson. Please don't be afraid. I won't hurt you. Please . . . I've come here to apologize. Don't be scared." He spoke slowly and quietly, as he began twisting his hat between his hands.

Eve hesitated. "An apology? I don't know what you mean."

"Yes," continued George, "it's about your painting . . . the one that was stolen. I did it. I'm the person who took it, but I didn't do it for myself. I was forced to do it."

Slowly, Eve began to regain her composure. She thought the man looked very sad, almost on the verge of tears. Even though she still had some misgivings, she opened the door wider. "Come inside," she said with a slight hesitation. "You can tell me what you're talking about."

Eve led George Gomez out to the patio. She thought it would be safer there than sitting inside the house, since she'd seen Frank working on his patio earlier. If she had to call for help, he would hear her and come to her aid.

"Sit down," Eve said calmly, pointing to a wrought-iron chair. Gomez did as he was told and she pulled up a chair in front of him. For some odd reason, this man looked familiar to her. She thought she'd seen him before—not at the restaurant, but somewhere else—but she didn't know where. "Now, tell me why you're here. Why do you owe me an apology?"

"As I said, I'm the person who stole your painting from the Sunshine Gallery, but it wasn't my idea. I didn't want to steal it. I was forced to do it. I used to work at the Crazy Cactus restaurant, as a waiter, and I also worked part-time at the art gallery. One day, Mr. Wolf called me into his office. He told me there was a painting in the gallery that he'd seen and wanted me to steal. At first, I refused. I told him I wasn't a thief. Then, he became very angry and threatened me. He said if I didn't do it, he'd fire me. I just couldn't let that happen, so I finally agreed to do what he wanted. He explained that he had been at the gallery's last exhibit, then described your painting and told me to take it. He knew that I also worked at the gallery and had easy access to your canvas. So, I just took it one day, when no one was looking, put it in my car, and brought it to the restaurant."

"That's where I saw you . . . at the Sunshine Gallery. I knew you looked familiar," responded Eve.

"Yes, but I don't work there any longer. Jack Slater, the owner, fired me when he found out what I'd done. Then, Mr. Wolf called me into his office again and said he wanted me to steal more paintings. When I refused, he fired me too. Now, I don't have any work and I have a family to care for. I don't know what I'm going to do." He was practically on the verge of tears as he spoke.

"Calm down, Mr. Gomez," said Eve softly. "Just tell me one thing. There are so many beautiful paintings in the Sunshine Gallery; why did Dick Wolf want my work? Did he like it so much that he had to steal it?"

"I don't think that was the reason. He simply said he had a blank space to fill on a wall in his restaurant. He said your canvas was the only one in the exhibit that looked like the right size."

"That's why he had you steal my painting . . . because of the size of the canvas?" Eve had to stifle a laugh. "What a joke! Here I thought somebody really liked my artistry."

"I'm sorry, but that's all he told me," responded the man, afraid that he'd misspoken.

"Okay, Mr. Gomez . . . George . . . don't worry. You can relax now. I accept your apology. I understand that you were forced to do something you wouldn't have done on your own. But, tell me this, if Dick Wolf fired you, what were you doing in his office yesterday?"

"He owed me some back pay...not much...but I need everything I can get. He called me in the morning and told me to come over to his office around noon. He said he had a check for me. So, that's exactly what I did. When I got there, I knocked on his door, but there was no answer, so I pushed it open. When I entered, I was shocked to see Mr. Wolf lying on the floor. I thought he was dead and it scared me to see him like that, so I just turned and got out of there as fast as I could."

"Why did you run when you saw me, my husband, and Maria?" asked Eve.

"I was afraid you would think I killed him. I wasn't thinking straight. I was so scared," replied George, as he began twisting the hat in his hands. "But, Mrs.

Iverson, you must believe me. I didn't kill Mr. Wolf. As I said, he was lying on the floor when I got there. Please believe me. I'm not a thief and I'm certainly not a killer."

"Call me Eve . . . and yes, I believe you. Did you tell the sheriff everything you just told me?"

"Yes. Two officers came to my home. They searched the house for a gun, but didn't find one. I don't own a gun. I've never owned a weapon. Then, the sheriff's men took me to the station. I was there for hours. They asked me all sorts of questions and did a lot of tests. I was afraid they were going to throw me in jail. Finally, they told me I was free to go, but not to leave town. Oh, Eve," he added, hesitatingly, "I have a wife and two children and very little money. I'm not going anywhere. All I want to do now is to clear my name. I don't want my children growing up thinking their father is a murderer."

As George recounted everything that he'd been through in the past twenty-four hours, Eve began to soften. Despite his anxiety, she sensed an underlying kindness in the man. She also thought he was very handsome and probably only in his late thirties. After listening to his explanation of events, she leaned over and touched his knee. "Thank you, George. It was very kind of you to come here today. Thank you for your apology and for telling me your story. You don't have to worry. I believe everything you just told me."

"I'm so glad. That makes me feel much better. I felt I had to talk to you, as soon as possible. I wanted to make things clear. I'm so sorry I stole your painting and I had to explain why I ran away when I saw the three of you coming towards Mr. Wolf's office." He leaned forward and pushed himself up from the chair. "Now . . . I'll be going. You're very kind to listen to me and allow me to take up so much of your time."

"Not at all. Please don't hesitate to let me know if there's anything I can do to help you in the future," responded Eve, as she led the man back into the house and out the front door.

Well, thought Eve, as she walked back to the patio, *that was unexpected. Either he's innocent, as he claims to be, or he's an awfully good actor.* She sat down at her easel and made a feeble attempt to continue where she'd left off. After about ten minutes of scratching some lines on the canvas, she stopped. Once again, Coco started barking and ran into the house. She turned and saw that Adam had returned. Following the dog's lead, Eve also went inside.

"How's the painting coming?" asked Adam. "Any new masterpieces?"

"I'm afraid not," replied Eve. "But, wait 'til you hear what I have to tell you. You'll never guess who I've been talking to since you left."

"Who's that?" Adam asked, innocently.

"George Gomez," responded Eve, tersely. She suspected that Adam would not have a positive reaction to her news and she was right.

"What? The man from the restaurant? The man we saw run out of Dick Wolf's office? The man who may be a killer?" gasped Adam. "You let him in the house? Are you okay? What did he want? Did he try to hurt you?" Suddenly, his voice became louder and filled with concern.

"Not to worry. I'm fine. We had a very nice talk and, I must say, I rather like him and feel sorry for what he's been through," Eve replied, calmly, then related the gist of her conversation with the unexpected visitor.

"I just wish I'd been here. I'm sorry you had to deal with him alone, but I'm glad you're okay." After a slight pause, he continued. "Now, it's my turn. I have a few things to tell you."

"Yes . . . I'm anxious to hear what the sheriff had to say. Tell me," Eve encouraged her husband.

As they sat down in the living room, Adam began to relate his latest news. "I learned quite a bit. They only asked me a few questions, which I thought we answered sufficiently when we gave our initial statements, but I answered them again anyway. Maybe they wanted to see if I'd tell the same story twice. Maybe they even thought we were the culprits."

"You're kidding," interrupted Eve. "I hope they don't think we killed Dick Wolf." *It was so like Adam*, she thought, *to make light of serious matters*.

"Well, they did ask about your stolen painting and suggested we might have been angry when we saw it hanging in the restaurant," Adam explained.

"I trust you set them straight."

"Yes, dear. I don't think we'll be arrested," Adam replied, then continued. "They brought in George Gomez and asked him questions. His story panned out. He told them he went to Dick Wolf's office to pick up a check and they found it in an unopened envelope on the desk. Neither blood nor gun powder residue were found on him, so they finally had to let him go. The only evidence they have is circumstantial. Nevertheless, he's still considered what is now called a 'person of interest' and they'll be keeping a close eye on him. Sheriff Warner told me that Dick Wolf was shot once in the chest, from a few feet away. The bullet went right through his heart. He probably died instantly. They dug a twenty-two caliber bullet out of his chest, but no weapon was discovered. They also found a letter opener in his right hand. They think he was either being attacked by someone and trying to defend himself, or he was threatening someone and the person shot him in self-defense. They still have to do an autopsy, but Sheriff Warner doesn't think there will be any surprises. From what I gathered, it seems as if our victim was quite an ogre. Apparently, he threatened a lot of people. The sheriff had met with him several times and had warned him to take it easy, but, because nobody ever pressed charges, nothing was ever done to stop him from harassing others. If you can believe it, he even had a wife—now a widow—and a step-daughter from a previous marriage. Not surprisingly, a divorce was in the works, but hadn't been finalized before he died. His widow lives here in Sunshine Valley and will inherit everything. As for the staff, even though so many were yelling out that they killed him, when questioned individually by the sheriff's men, they all maintained their innocence. So, bottom line is that, after interviewing almost a hundred people, both employees and customers, they don't have a real suspect and, I fear, they won't find one either. It appears that too many people had both a motive and the opportunity to do away with Mr. Wolf."

"I'm surprised Sheriff Warner shared so much information with you," replied Eve.

"I don't think he told me anything confidential. He said he could only tell me some basic facts. He trusts us and knows we won't talk to the media or engage in gossip," replied Adam.

"That's for sure," agreed Eve, then continued. "Maybe it's because we saw him running away that I initially thought George Gomez might have been the killer. But, after talking with him and now, based on what you learned, I'm pretty sure he didn't do it. Someone else put an end to the big, bad wolf, as the restaurant staff referred to him. Did the sheriff tell you if anyone in the restaurant heard a gun shot?"

"No. Nobody ... neither customers nor employees... seem to have heard anything resembling a gun shot, but, it was very noisy in the dining room. I doubt that anyone would have paid attention, even if a bomb had gone off."

"Any one of the people who were in the restaurant could be the killer," remarked Eve. "Maybe several people worked together as a team. It certainly sounds like quite a few folks had both motive and opportunity to commit murder."

"Well," added Adam, "you could be right. I don't envy Sheriff Warner. I think he has his hands full and it'll take quite a while to wrap up this case, if that's even possible."

"Did he say he wanted to talk to me?" Eve asked hesitatingly.

"No, just don't try to leave town," replied Adam with a smile.

"Very funny . . . not funny. I may have to go to Tucson on some errands, but I'll try to stay close to home. I'd hate for Sheriff Warner to have to send a posse after me. Now," continued Eve, as she changed the subject, "I don't think I want to paint today, after all. If you're going to be home, I'd like to take the car and drive over to the Sunshine Gallery. I have a few questions about my painting and I want to talk to Jack Slater."

Adam gave his wife a serious look. "I hope you're not going to get any more involved with this mess." From all their years of being together, he knew it was pointless to try and dissuade Eve from doing something, once she had her mind made up.

"No, dear, not to worry. I just have a few simple questions about my stolen painting. Everything happened so quickly, I never really had an opportunity to find out more about the theft. So . . . is it okay to take the car? I won't be very long."

"Sure. I wasn't planning on going anywhere. I want to get back to my stamp research. Take your time."

"Great. I'll just put away my paints," replied Eve and walked out to her patio studio. She looked at her drawing and smiled broadly. Pleased with the start she'd made, she turned, re-entered the house, and grabbed her purse.

"See you later," she called to Adam, then exited.

As Eve drove to the Sunshine Gallery, she tried to keep focused on the road and enjoy the serene desert landscape that surrounded her. She wasn't quite sure how to deal with Jack Slater. She had questions for him about her stolen painting and the involvement of George Gomez, but wanted to be as tactful as possible and not upset him. Pulling into the quiet parking lot, she immediately found an empty space.

When she entered the gallery, Eve noticed that there was only one large painting hanging on a wall. "Jack? Are you here?" she shouted, as she walked around the outer room.

Clad in his usual western outfit, the gallery owner emerged from his office. "Hi, Eve. Good to see you again," he said and smiled. "How are things going? I hope you're still painting."

"Not to worry. I'm churning them out every day and have done so many that, I'm afraid I'm running out of space to hang anything more in my house. Even the storeroom is getting crowded." *Remember*, she thought, *take it slowly and be tactful.* "Actually, the reason I'm here is that I have a couple of questions I'd like to ask you," she said, in her most casual tone.

"Of course," replied Jack. "Ask away. I don't know if I have the answers you're looking for, but try me."

"First of all, George Gomez came to see me this morning. He told me everything . . . how he was forced by Dick Wolf to steal my painting. He was very apologetic. We talked for quite a while and I found myself feeling very sorry for him. He told me he was fired from his job at the Crazy Cactus and then, he told me you let him go as well. He has a family to care for and was very distraught. I'm curious. When did you find out that he was the thief and why didn't you want to tell me?"

"Actually," said Jack, "I was going to tell you . . . yesterday, as a matter of fact. However, when I heard about the murder of Dick Wolf and that you and Adam were the ones who discovered the body, I thought it best to wait a bit until things quieted down. I thought you had probably seen and heard enough for one day and the news about your stolen..."

Eve didn't let him finish. "You did? You heard about us? Where? Who told you?"

"As you know, this is a small town," replied Jack. "When something as terrible as a murder happens, word spreads quickly. Several people stopped by the gallery and told me the news. As for George Gomez, I deduced that he was the person most likely to steal a painting from my gallery, so I confronted him one day. He admitted it and, as he told you, he said it wasn't his idea, but that he was forced to do it. I've always liked George and I believed what he told me. Nevertheless, I had no choice but to let him go."

"Oh, Jack. He's so remorseful and he really needs work. Don't you think, under the circumstances, that you could re-hire him?"

The man had a very sheepish look on his face, as he slowly replied. "I really can't do that, even if I wanted to. If people found out that an art thief was working here, nobody would want to show their paintings or even come in . . . and, I'm sure that people would find out. Furthermore, if my insurance company discovered that I had a thief working here, they'd cancel me . . . and now, there's even a suggestion that George might be the one who killed Dick Wolf. I hope it's not true, but the rumor is out there."

"He didn't do it," Eve replied brusquely. "He's not a killer. Of that, I'm positive."

"I too want to believe he didn't do it. I know that awful man had many enemies. Even I had a run in with him," said Jack. "When I went to the restaurant yesterday to confront him, he really let me have it."

"You did what?" gasped Eve. "You were at the restaurant yesterday? Why? What time? Did you see or hear anything?"

"I was there before the heavy lunch crowd, just as people were starting to arrive," replied Jack. "I didn't look at my watch, so I'm not sure exactly what time it was. I went there to tell Dick Wolf never to come to my gallery again, or I'd call the sheriff. I'd seen him in here a few times and I remember asking him if he was interested in purchasing a painting. He just rebuffed me and said they were too expensive. When I went to his office, I told him I knew that he was the one responsible for stealing your painting and that I was going to report him. He just laughed, then yelled at me to get out, or he'd report me. That was the end of our confrontation. I just turned and went out. The restaurant was beginning to fill up. I didn't see or hear anything unusual, but, I assure you, he was very much alive when I left him."

"Did you tell the sheriff that you were at the restaurant?" Eve asked, in disbelief.

"No. It really didn't seem necessary. I didn't have anything noteworthy to tell him and I was reluctant to get involved. I had every intention of reporting the man for the theft, but, later, when I heard the news, I thought it was useless and decided to keep quiet. In the end, I believe, as do a lot of other people, that he got what he deserved."

"I don't blame you for feeling the way you do. I just wish Adam and I weren't involved. Now, our names will be connected with Dick Wolf's murder. But, so be it. There's nothing we can do about it now."

Eve was getting ready to leave the gallery, when Jack stopped her.

"You know, Eve, there's one other reason I wanted to talk to you," he began. "I was wondering if we could arrange to have another exhibit of your paintings . . . this time, a one-woman show . . . that is, if you aren't too turned off by what happened to one of your paintings in the last exhibit. I really admire your work and would like to do you justice. What do you think? Is it possible that we could work together again?"

"You must be reading my mind. I was kind of hoping that might be a possibility. I've been doing so much painting lately and have so many canvases. I don't know what to do with all of them. You haven't seen my latest efforts. I've changed my style and it may not be what you had in mind. I've been doing more landscapes . . . mainly in the style of Fritz Scholder . . . I'm not copying him, just using him for inspiration."

"Don't worry," replied Jack. "I trust your artistic judgment and, I must say, I'm also a great admirer of his work, both his American Indian portraits and his landscapes. If you agree, I'm hoping we can do this sooner, rather than later. I'd like to have a showing of your work before all the tourists and part-time residents leave town for the summer . . . let's say, in a couple of weeks. I was thinking we could have a two-week exhibit . . . starting on Saturday the seventh . . . that's lucky seven," he said, looking at a calendar. "We could also arrange to have an artist's reception on the opening day, where you would be present and folks could come and talk with you. What do you think? Are you game?"

"Wow," responded Eve. "I was thinking of the fall, but I agree, the sooner the better. I can have Adam help me bring over some canvases. How many do you think you'd like? I'm sure I have enough."

"That depends. What are the sizes?"

"I haven't done anything very large yet. They're all pretty much similar to the ones you saw . . . medium sized . . . 24 x 30 and 29 x 24."

"I'd say we could easily handle about twenty. Do you have that many?"

Eve laughed. "You bet . . . and then some. It will be good to get them out of the house."

"Great," replied Jack. "Why don't you bring over what you have done so far and we can do some pricing. How about three days from today? Do you think that gives you enough time?"

"Not a problem. If we're going to have an exhibit, there's one other thing I'd like to ask you," Eve said, hesitatingly.

"Yes, I think I know what you're thinking. No, I won't be able to have George Gomez help me . . . I explained why and I hope you understand my reasons. His presence would keep a lot of folks away from your exhibit, or even draw them here, but for the wrong reasons. I'll get help from my nephew, though. He's staying with me now and is eager to become involved with the gallery. You haven't met him, but I think you're going to like Tommy. He's a real art lover and I know he'll appreciate your work."

"Again, you were reading my mind," responded Eve. "I better watch myself. I understand your reasons for not bringing George back. It does make me sad, however. I just wish there was something I could do to help him. But, I look forward to meeting your nephew."

"I know how you feel, but we have to get on with our own lives. I think we should be able to draw a large crowd and, hopefully, sell some of your art work."

"Okay. I can't wait to go home and tell Adam the good news. We'll be back in a few days with some masterpieces." Eve turned and exited the gallery. *What a pleasant surprise*, she thought, as she smiled and got into her car.

On her way home, Eve began reviewing in her mind all the paintings she had completed to date. Although she admired the skill of artists who painted realistically, she didn't feel the style was right for her and her output was becoming increasingly abstract. She enjoyed giving her own interpretation to objects and scenes and she preferred working with shapes and colors, rather than attempting to duplicate realistic settings.

After pulling into her driveway, she jumped out of the car and ran into the house. As usual, Coco was there to greet her and began barking and running in circles around her. "Oh, Adam, have I got news for you," she called out to her husband, who was just emerging from the den.

"I hope it's not more trouble," he said, somberly.

"No, dear, just the opposite," responded Eve. "As I told you, I went to the Sunshine Gallery and spoke with Jack Slater. He wants to have another showing of my paintings . . . before everyone leaves town for the summer." She thought it best not to mention anything to her husband about the conversation she'd had with Jack regarding George Gomez and the theft of the painting from a previous show, or that he went to the restaurant to confront Dick Wolf.

"That's great. I was worried that you might be getting more involved with the murder. I'm so pleased. Let me know what help you need. I'm always here to be of assistance to a famous artist."

"Well, I don't think I'd call myself famous . . . at least, not yet," she said, with a laugh. "Once again, a day that started out on a sad note ended up being positive. Now that I'm so inspired, I think I'll go back to my studio and see if there's anything else I can turn out."

The remainder of the day was quiet. Eve threw herself into her art work and Adam went into the den to continue doing stamp research on his computer. After everything the Iversons had been through, they were grateful that the phone didn't ring and no one came to the door. Even Coco seemed calmer.

Chapter 4

The Iversons spent the following two days without interruption, assembling the paintings that were to be shown at Eve's exhibit. On the third day, they both awakened earlier than usual and went into the kitchen to enjoy their morning toast and coffee.

"Well," said Adam, as he sat across from Eve at the table, "it looks like we're getting a bit more peace around here. You certainly seem to be sleeping better and I know I am. Even Coco appears calmer."

"I've started playing my word games again when I go to bed," replied Eve. "They help me avoid thinking about everything that's happened during the day. Lately, when I lie down and am horizontal, for some reason, all sorts of thoughts—good and bad—start popping into my head and prevent me from falling into a nice, deep sleep. The games are wonderful and really help me clear my mind."

"Word games? What do you mean?" asked Adam, quizzically. "I don't hear you saying anything."

"You wouldn't hear me. They're mental games. I thought I told you. Anyway, in one of my games, I try to go through the alphabet, starting from A, all the way to Z, and think of words that might end in -*est*. For example, *attest, behest, contest, detest, etcetera, etcetera*. Get it? If I finish, I'll start over and try to think of words that have other endings like -*ion*, -*ate*, and so forth. It works really well and I usually fall asleep somewhere in the middle, or towards the end of the alphabet."

"Yes . . . I remember you telling me . . . sounds like a neat trick . . . and you don't need to take any medication," replied Adam.

"I was also inspired by Jackie to play another game," added Eve.

"Jackie? What does she have to do with your games?" Adam asked, with raised eyebrows.

"Well, the day we first met her at Frank's barbecue, she said that, when she was little, she used to be teased by other children who claimed she had a boy's name. Now, if I get into bed and want to clear my head, I go through the alphabet and try to think of names that can apply to both males and females. Last night, I thought of quite a few and slumbered off with *Pat*. You should try playing a mental word game whenever you're having difficulty falling asleep. It really helps shut out any unpleasant thoughts you might be carrying with you."

"My dear, as I've told you many times, you're very clever," said Adam.

"Words have always fascinated me. As you know, that's why I became a language teacher. Words can be both good and bad. They can make people happy or sad . . . even angry. They can even be deadly. I've been thinking a lot about words since Dick Wolf's demise and, you know what conclusion I've come to? I have a very strong suspicion that his own words may have played a role in his death. From all we've been hearing, his words were mostly bad and very hurtful. He made a lot of people angry with his insults and threats. I wouldn't be surprised if his killer might have been a victim of his nasty words at some point and wanted revenge." Eve continued sipping her coffee.

"You may very well be right . . . it does make sense," replied Adam.

"I remember a professor I once taught with," mused Eve. "Like Dick Wolf, he was very mean. All he could do was criticize and find fault with everything and everyone. He did this almost daily and I always did my best to avoid him. He was really hated by the rest of the faculty. Although he was never killed by anyone, if he had been, he wouldn't have been missed. I don't understand why some people have to be so unpleasant."

"Perhaps it's the way they were brought up," suggested Adam.

"Well," replied Eve, "I wish they'd grow out of it when they become adults. This is why I don't particularly like watching the news. There's so much meanness and cruelty in the world and I don't want to see it or hear about it."

"Speaking of the news," remarked Adam, "I haven't heard much more about Dick Wolf's murder. Although no arrests have been made yet, they're still keeping an eye on the same person of interest."

"Oh . . . poor George," sighed Eve. "I wonder how he's doing. He was so upset when he came here and told me his story. I wish there was something I could do to help him. Maybe I should at least give him a call and let him know I'm thinking of him."

"Please don't," said Adam, firmly. "I know how kind you are and I don't like to tell you what to do, but I hope you won't get more involved with this case. It's not good for your mental or emotional health. The past couple of days have been nice and quiet and I'd like it to stay that way. I'm sure you would too. Remember, we didn't move to this beautiful oasis to get involved with murder."

"You're right," replied Eve, as she hit the table with her empty cup. "Besides, we have other things to do. Let's get going. I think it's time to bring my paintings over to the gallery. I know Jack is expecting us."

After finishing their breakfast, Adam and Eve began carrying an assortment of canvases out to the car. "Are you sure you have enough?" teased Adam, after placing the last one in the trunk.

"If not, I certainly have many more. We'll see what Jack says."

As they drove to the gallery, Eve began staring out the window. Leaning back in her seat, she turned to her husband and began to speak in a soft voice. "Say, Adam, do you think we could go for a ride up into the mountains one of these days? I'd like to take some photographs. So far, most of the scenes I've painted depict the landscape from my perspective down here. I'd like to see how the desert looks from another angle...somewhere high in the mountains. I'm sure there are quite a few different shapes that I could paint."

"We can do that," replied Adam, "and maybe even get in some hiking while we're at it."

"Or a little sky diving," added Eve.

"We'll save that until we're older," countered Adam, as they both laughed.

Once again, the parking lot was empty and Adam immediately found a space in front of Sunshine Gallery.

"Jack told me his nephew has moved in with him now and will be eager to help with the exhibit. I wonder if he's here today." Eve had no sooner finished speaking, when two men emerged from the gallery and approached the car.

"Howdy, Adam and Eve," said Jack, as he tipped his cowboy hat. A younger man followed closely behind him. He was dressed in jeans and a white tee shirt that boasted a picture of one of Andy Warhol's soup cans on the front. "I want you to meet my nephew, Tommy. He'll be helping us today . . . and, in the future, I'm happy to say." They all shook hands, then began unloading the canvases from the car. Since there were four of them, it only took one trip.

Once inside, Jack began looking through Eve's paintings. "These are perfect. I'm very impressed with what you've done since the last exhibit," he said. "I think folks are going to like your work, as well. I'm quite sure we'll have a very successful show." Then, turning to his nephew, he asked, "What do you think, Tommy? Do you agree?"

"Yes! They're terrific. I love your style . . . great shapes and colors," replied the young man.

"My work is gradually becoming more abstract," replied Eve. "I really enjoy the look and I'm so pleased you both like what I've done as well."

"Most of your paintings appear to be of the desert, but I see you've also done a couple of water scenes," said Tommy, as he began arranging the canvases.

"That's because Adam and I used to live in San Diego and we loved to walk along the beach. Even though I love Sunshine Valley, I do miss the ocean. So, if I can't get there now, I thought I'd bring the water to me, here in the desert," replied Eve.

"Very clever," said Tommy. "I think some folks who live here might feel the same way."

"In the meantime, while Tommy starts hanging the paintings, we can discuss pricing," said Jack, as his nephew began arranging the canvases. "My thought is this . . . since they're all about the same size, if we say five hundred dollars for you, I'll add a standard forty percent for the gallery. That makes a sales price of seven hundred dollars per painting. I'd like to charge more, but, for now, I think we need to wait until you develop a reputation, before we go over a thousand dollars. Are you with me on this?"

"That sounds good to me," replied Eve. "I trust your judgment. I'm not out to make a lot of money . . . at least, not yet. I'll be very satisfied with whatever we're able to sell . . . even one painting would do it. What about you? Do you have any thoughts?" she asked, as she turned to Adam.

"Nope. This really isn't my field. I'll go with whatever Jack suggests," answered her husband.

"I wish everyone were this easy to work with," added Jack, with a laugh. "I think we're on a roll here. We'll get busy and hang the paintings. But first, I want to frame them . . . just something simple. A frame always settles a painting. By that, I mean it increases the aesthetic appeal and helps the viewer focus. I'll also get the word out about the exhibit. As we discussed, the artist's reception will be on Saturday the seventh and will run from two to five in the afternoon. I'm sure a lot of folks will want to meet and talk with you."

"I'll be there . . . I'm looking forward to it," responded Eve.

As they left the gallery and began to drive home, Eve turned to Adam and mused. "The reception should be interesting, but I wonder what people are going to ask me. I've never done anything like this before. I certainly haven't been required to talk to people about my art work or my background. Let's hope I have the answers to their questions."

"I'm not the least bit concerned and you shouldn't be either. Knowing you as well as I do, I doubt that you'll have any difficulty. Just be honest and say what you believe and feel. I think people will be interested in anything you have to say," replied Adam, reassuringly.

"Well, I hope you're right. I'm sure somebody is going to ask me where I learned how to paint and if I have a degree in art. Did I take art courses somewhere? Have I exhibited in other galleries? The simple answer is 'none of the above.' I once had to take an art class in high school, but I don't think that counts. Basically, I'm self taught."

"That's even better. It gives inspiration to others who'd like to paint, but, like you, have little, or no, formal training," replied Adam.

"True. I've always enjoyed going to museums and art galleries and I know a lot of famous artists started painting on their own . . . for example, Frida Kahlo, Winslow Homer, Grandma Moses, and Paul Gauguin were all self taught and I love what they did."

"Well, then, it's safe to say that you're in good company," said Adam, with a smile. "I don't think there's anything you need to worry about. Your work speaks for itself."

After a short pause, Eve continued, "I must say, Jack's nephew seemed nice. He certainly appears to like art. Did you see what he was wearing? Maybe you should start . . . never mind."

"Thank you," said Adam. "Anyway, I much prefer Jack's wardrobe."

"Yes, I know. The two of you make a good pair . . . all you need now are some spurs," replied Eve, teasingly.

"Once I get a horse," countered Adam, with a smile.

"I wonder if Tommy went with Jack to Dick Wolf's office. They seem very close," continued Eve. Suddenly, she wished she could take back her words. She didn't mean to tell Adam that she knew Jack had been at the restaurant.

"What? You didn't tell me that. Jack was at the office? The day of the murder?" asked Adam, in surprise.

"I didn't want to tell you. I thought it might upset you," replied Eve.

"It doesn't matter . . . whether he went alone or with Tommy . . . don't you go there. Try not to think about the Wolf affair any more. Your main concern now is your art work. Just focus on the exhibit and make a very big effort to put everything regarding the murder out of your mind. You don't need it."

"You're right," replied Eve. "As a matter of fact, I think I'm going to go for a swim when we get home. I haven't been to the pool in quite a while and I feel I could use some exercise. I've been sitting too much lately."

"That's more like it," said Adam, then squeezed her leg.

"Do you want to come with me?" asked Eve.

"Not today. I thought I'd take Coco and go over and visit with Frank for a bit. We haven't talked in quite a while and I want to see how he's doing. It's ironic. I saw more of him when Olive was alive. I think he's been very busy with a lot of outside things he couldn't do when she was hovering over him."

Once they arrived home, Eve went into the bedroom and slipped into her bathing suit and terrycloth robe, as she prepared to go to the pool. "It's been a long time, but I'm going to see if I can still do a few laps," she said to her husband, who was waiting in the hallway.

After attaching Coco's leash, Adam and Eve exited the house, each heading in separate directions.

"Have a good swim," said Adam, over his shoulder, "and take your time. We're not going anywhere."

Walking towards the pool, Eve smiled, pleased with what she had accomplished. While she'd planned on doing some painting after moving to Sunshine Valley, she never dreamt that she would be having a one-woman exhibit of her work . . . and so soon.

As she reached the pool, two bicyclists passed her and waved. Upon opening the gate, she noticed that the area was relatively empty. *Good*, she thought, *it's not as crowded as the mornings*. Only one woman was in the pool. Looking around, she saw another woman in a lounge chair begin to wave at her.

"Eve . . . over here. Come and sit by me," the woman called out. It was Peggy Walsh, a regular at the pool.

Even though she was wearing a broad-brimmed hat that partly covered her face, Eve recognized the woman immediately and walked over to her. "Hi, Peggy. You look very cozy. Let me pull up a chair and I'll join you," she said, as she made herself comfortable.

"I've missed you. It's been a while, but I know you've been busy," said Peggy, with a chuckle.

"Yes, I have and I certainly need the exercise," replied Eve.

The woman in the pool continued swimming, then stopped and paddled over to the stairs. She climbed out of the water, grabbed her towel, and began wiping her hair.

"Jackie, is it you?" called Eve, from where she was seated.

"Yes, it is," replied the woman, as she walked towards Eve and continued drying her hair. Her skin glistened and a few black tendrils clung to her forehead.

"I'm really impressed. I was watching you swim. You're good. You look like you're just about ready for the Olympics," said Eve, as she smiled at the woman.

"Thank you. This is a very nice pool. I might have to put off the Olympics for a while, but, now that I'm getting more settled, you'll be seeing me here on a daily basis," replied Jackie, with a laugh.

"Why don't you come and sit by us. I'd like you to meet Peggy. She's a pool regular," said Eve.

"Give me a minute," replied Jackie. "Let me bring my things over here. I'll be right back." She walked around the edge of the pool to her chair, then picked up her bag, slipped into her sandals, and returned to the two women.

"You can sit here," said Eve, as she pulled over an empty chair.

"Phew. That was a real workout," said Jackie, as she sat down and gave her hair another couple of pats with the towel.

"Jackie, this is Peggy . . . Peggy, I'd like you to meet Jackie Quinn. She's a newcomer to our beautiful valley," said Eve, as she introduced the two women to each other.

"I must say," said Peggy, as she smiled at Jackie, "I'm also impressed with your swimming. How many laps did you do? I got tired just watching you and stopped counting after ten."

"I think it was fifteen today, but my goal is thirty, or even more. Swimming is one of the best exercises a person can do and it helps get the kinks out of my sore muscles. I just love it. It's so refreshing."

"And you, Eve?" Peggy looked at her friend. "I expect you've been busy too. I heard about your last escapade at the Crazy Cactus. That must have been quite a shock for you . . . discovering a dead body. . ."

The woman was interrupted by Eve, before she could finish. "How did you hear about that?" she asked.

"I'm afraid word gets around very quickly here, especially when it has to do with a murder. Anyway, I wanted to tell you that I was at the restaurant that day, as well."

"You were there?" asked Eve, in surprise.

"Yes. I was having lunch with my niece and her two children. We were just about finished, when I saw you and Adam come in. I waved, but you didn't see me. You were walking towards the rear, behind a woman. After the three of you found the body of Dick Wolf, she must have gone and told some of the other employees.

They probably passed on the news to a few of the regular customers. It didn't take long before everything in the dining room became rather chaotic, but it was mostly the employees who began running around and making all the noise. We wanted to leave, but our waiter told us we had to remain seated until the authorities arrived."

"Did you see or hear anything unusual . . . like a gun shot?" continued Eve.

"Just some banging of pots and pans in the kitchen... nothing that sounded like a gun shot. At one point, a little earlier, before you came in, I went to the ladies room in the back of the restaurant with one of my niece's daughters. As we passed Mr. Wolf's office . . . I think it was his office . . . I did notice a woman who was just coming out."

"Did you see what she looked like?" persisted Eve.

"I didn't really pay much attention. I think she wore glasses and had short white hair, but I can't tell you what her clothes looked like. She was sort of nondescript and we were in a hurry," continued Peggy.

"Did you tell the sheriff what you saw?" Eve asked.

"I told the officer who came to our table, but I didn't have much to say, other than what I just told you," added Peggy. "I wouldn't recognize her if my life depended on it. My main concern was the children. I was so sorry they had to be part of all the chaos. They were very confused and didn't understand what was happening. Fortunately, as soon as we answered all the officer's questions, we were allowed to leave. We didn't even have to pay for our lunch."

"This is unbelievable," said Eve. "It seems that everyone I talk to was at the Crazy Cactus that day . . . even Jackie here."

"Yes," replied Jackie, as she leaned forward, "but earlier. I went to pick up some flan. I wasn't there very long and I didn't see or hear anything strange. I was quite surprised when I heard the news report on the radio. I think all the mayhem occurred after I left . . . thank goodness."

"Well," added Peggy, "I hope they find the culprit sooner, rather than later. Even though I've heard that a lot of folks are glad Dick Wolf is gone, I hate to think that there's a killer running loose in Sunshine Valley. I've been watching the news and keep hearing that they have a person of interest who's being looked at. They haven't given out any names, or made any arrests, but everyone knows that a former employee, George Gomez, is the person they're talking about."

"You're right, Peggy, word certainly does get around fast. On a brighter note," said Eve, eager to change the subject. "I have to tell you both some exciting news. Believe it or not, I'm going to have a one-woman art show at the Sunshine Gallery." She went on to tell the two women about the exhibit that was to take place.

"That's fabulous," said Peggy. "I'll be sure to go there."

"Me too," added Jackie. "I love art and I can't wait to see what you've done . . . But, right now, if you two will excuse me, I have to be going. Frank is supposed to come over to my house and do some weeding and planting in my patio garden. I have so much work to do in my new house and he's been very helpful. But, I'll be seeing you again soon . . . so nice to meet you Peggy." She rose from her chair, collected her swimming gear, pulled on a long, cotton smock, then made her way to the exit.

"Lovely woman," said Peggy. "Even though I just paddle around in the shallow water and don't really swim, I love to watch those who do. I must say, we have quite a few excellent swimmers here. Now, it's your turn."

"Just what I had in mind. It's been a while, so don't expect a lot and please don't compare me to Jackie," replied Eve with a laugh, as she made her way to the pool. Out of the corner of her eye, she saw a couple of people look at her and whisper to each other, but she tried not to think about it.

After crossing the length of the pool several times, Eve swam to the shallow end and pushed herself up and out of the water. "Well," she said to Peggy, "that'll do it for today. I'm a bit out of shape, but, I can assure you, I'll be back again soon."

"I hope so . . . and, if I don't see you before your exhibit, I'll certainly see you at the gallery," replied Peggy, as Eve began drying herself.

When she left the pool area and began walking home, Eve reviewed in her mind what she'd just heard from Jackie and smiled at the thought of her and Frank. She was sure a close relationship was developing between the two of them and was happy for Frank.

Once inside her house, Eve headed for the bathroom, took a shower, dried herself, and then put on some clean clothes. She rolled up her wet suit and towel and went out to the patio to hang them up. Looking over to Frank's house, she saw Adam and Coco, who were making their way home.

"Have a nice swim?" asked Adam, as he entered the patio. "How many laps did you do today? Fifty? A hundred?"

"Yes, I had a good swim and I did so many laps, I lost count," replied Eve. "Let's sit down. I have something to tell you," she added, in a serious tone.

"Likewise," replied Adam, as he unleashed the dog.

"But, first, I think we should share our news over a drink," said Eve.

"Good idea . . . white wine okay?"

"Perfect," replied Eve, as she made herself comfortable in one of the patio chairs.

Adam returned shortly, handed a glass to his wife, and then took a seat opposite her. "You go first," he said.

"Well, when I was at the pool, I ran into Peggy Walsh and Jackie. First, it seems that Peggy was also at the restaurant when Dick Wolf was killed, but, she said she didn't notice or hear anything unusual."

"That really seems to be a popular place with folks here," replied Adam.

"Then, Jackie told me she had to leave because Frank was coming over to her house, to help with her gardening. She looked very happy when she mentioned his name. I'll bet something is developing between the two of them. Did Frank say anything to you about her?"

"He sure did," replied Adam. "That's what I wanted to tell you. First, he told me that he thinks Jackie would make a fun golf partner and he wants to teach her how to play the game. He said they've already played a few rounds of miniature golf and she beat him twice. He thinks she has a good eye."

"I'll say. She's got her eye on Frank, that's for sure."

"Then . . . wait 'til you hear this one," continued Adam. "He told me he's going to ask Jackie to go with him on a cruise to Alaska."

"How lovely. I've heard that's a beautiful cruise. But, what about Doty and Paula? Do you think they'll be upset that they're not included?" asked Eve.

"Actually, Frank told me that he did ask them if they also wanted to go on the cruise, but Paula said she gets seasick and Doty doesn't want to leave her alone. So, it will just be the two of them. He's going to ask Jackie today."

"It sounds like their relationship is becoming more and more serious," said Eve. "I hope everything works out okay. After everything Frank went through with Olive, he deserves someone nice, and Jackie certainly appears to fill the bill. She doesn't seem at all like the person Doty described . . . so shy and withdrawn. I think she's headed in a new direction in her second half of life."

"It appears that Frank is emerging from his shell as well," mused Adam. "But, I wonder about Jackie. I've had a few second thoughts. She seems unusually perky. I know her upbeat mood could be due to her move here and to meeting Frank, but I wonder if she isn't on some sort of medication. When I was working at the hospital, even though I was in administration, I saw quite a few people who, despite numerous problems, were always unusually upbeat. It turned out they were on meds to help elevate their mood. I think this is a common phenomenon, especially as people get older."

"Perhaps you're right," responded Eve. "She does seem very cheerful and full of energy. I remember once, when I was trying to lose weight, I got a prescription for some diet pills from a doctor. I thought it was a quick and easy way to drop a few pounds, but I just took one pill and thought I was going crazy. All of a sudden, I felt a spurt of energy rush through my whole body. I felt like I could do anything and kept busy all day . . . and night. I couldn't even go to sleep. I just wanted to keep moving and doing things . . . anything... just to keep moving. Then, when it wore off, I became so incredibly tired. All I wanted to do was sleep. I went to bed and slept for fifteen hours. That was the beginning and the absolute end of my drug career. After taking that one pill, I threw the rest away. I thought eating less and exercising more were safer than taking pills. But, if Jackie is on any medication, it's none of our business. She probably has a good reason for doing so. I think I could use something once in a while to relieve my anxieties, but, based on past experience, I'm afraid to try anything."

"Deep breathing and meditation . . . it's better for you than drugs . . . and much safer," said Adam, firmly.

"Yes, doctor," replied Eve, with a smile. "You don't have to worry. The diet pill experience was more than enough for me."

"In the meantime," continued Adam, "I have every intention of using you and Frank as my role models. I've been putting off gardening for too long and really must do some weeding and planting. I also want to get more exercise and, I must say, I'm very impressed with your swimming. I'm tired of just doing pushups in the house. So, tomorrow, I'm going to join a gym. There's a small one in town and I think it would be perfect for what I need. They have treadmills, exercycles, and some weights."

"Well, listen to you. Where is all this newly found energy coming from?" asked Eve, smiling.

"As I said, I'm going to be using you and Frank as my role models."

"And the gardening? When were you planning on fitting that into your schedule?" asked Eve, with a smile.

"Tomorrow . . . there's always tomorrow. The weeds will still be there," replied Adam, after taking another sip of wine. "Speaking of which, I almost forgot. Doty called and invited us to their house tomorrow afternoon. Frank and Jackie will be there, as well. I accepted for both of us."

Eve mumbled something resembling an agreement.

Looking over at his wife, Adam noticed a familiar expression on her face. *She's not thinking about Jackie and Frank*, he thought. She's not even thinking about her art work or her upcoming exhibit. It's George Gomez and the murder of Dick Wolf that are preoccupying her. But, based on past experience, he knew that nothing he could say, or do, would change Eve's mind. He just hoped she'd soon be able to put these thoughts aside and not get involved in any trouble.

Just then, the phone rang. "Stay here. I'll get it," said Adam, as he pushed himself out of the chair and quickly walked into the house.

After a few minutes, he returned to the patio.

"Well, that was a short one," commented Eve.

"It was a reporter from the local television station. He asked if we were the couple who found Dick Wolf's body and, if so, could they come and do an interview."

"I hope you said no," responded Eve, angrily.

"I told him he had the wrong number and then hung up. No way do I want reporters coming to the house. I certainly don't want to be interviewed for television and I know you're with me on that one."

"Absolutely. Well, at least he had the courtesy to call first and not show up on our doorstep with a camera crew," said Eve.

"I think there's a lot of talk going around and, I'm afraid we're becoming a big part of it. I'm quite certain Sheriff Warner didn't release our names. Someone else must have given them out, probably one of the employees at the restaurant."

With Coco stretched out between them, the couple continued enjoying their wine, but they were both deep in thought and remained quiet until it was time to go inside.

Chapter 5

Once again, Eve and Adam spent a quiet, restful night and they both awakened early, the following morning.

"So," said Eve, as Adam put on a sport shirt, "I see it's off to the gym this morning."

"Yes. I think it'll be good for me. If possible, I'd like to make it a daily routine . . . just for forty-five minutes or an hour . . . not too strenuous. And you? What are your plans? I won't be long, if you need to use the car."

"No, I'm not planning on going anywhere. I want to do some more painting. I'm very inspired now," replied Eve. "But first," she said as she finished combing her hair, "some breakfast," then went into the kitchen to prepare a quick meal for the two of them.

After downing a small bowl of oatmeal, Adam grabbed his hat and headed for the door. "I'll let you know how much weight I can lift," he said, as he left the house.

Once she cleared the dishes and put some water and food down for Coco, Eve walked out to the patio to resume her painting. As she looked around, she noticed several hummingbirds pecking at the feeder. "Oh dear, I haven't fed you in quite a while," she said, then went into the storeroom to get some bird food.

When she returned to the feeder that hung near the front entrance to the patio and began scattering a handful of seeds, she noticed two women approaching her house. One of the women had short, gray hair and wore glasses. The other woman, a blond, seemed much younger. She didn't recognize either one of them. "Can I help you?" Eve asked, when she realized they were headed for the front door.

"Mrs. Iverson?" asked the older of the two women. They walked over to the gate where Eve was standing. "I hope we're not disturbing you. I'm Valerie Wallace and this is Donna Bates. I'm Dick Wolf's widow and Donna is my surrogate daughter. I've been eager to meet you. Perhaps I should've called first, but I really wanted to talk with you in person. Not only do I owe you an apology, but I would also like to thank you and your husband."

Eve looked quizzically at the woman, then opened the gate. "Please come in. I'm not sure I understand you correctly," she responded, reluctantly, as the two women stepped carefully over the threshold and entered the patio. "You can sit outside, if you like . . . over here," she added, pointing to some chairs.

The women followed Eve's lead and sat down, with Coco following quietly behind. Wagging her tail, she propped herself up on a pillow. "Now," said Eve, "please tell me what this is all about."

The older woman leaned forward and slowly began to speak. "First, I want to apologize for the theft of your painting. I know that my ex-husband was responsible for stealing it and it's really shameful. Second, I want to thank you for finding his body. From what I've been hearing, everyone who knew him is glad he's gone. I'm sorry to have to say so, but that also includes both me and Donna."

"You don't need to thank me," replied Eve, as she felt the color drain from her face. "It was purely accidental that my husband Adam and I happened to be in the wrong place at the wrong time. We went to the restaurant to enjoy a nice lunch and when we noticed my painting hanging on the wall, we were just interested in talking with Mr. Wolf to find out how it came to be there. Maria, the assistant hostess, led us back to his office and that's where we saw him . . . on the floor."

"I understand, but, still, I'm grateful and very relieved. It may sound unkind of me, but, now that he's no longer here, everything is much easier. You have no idea how difficult life has been these past few years," the woman said, meekly.

"If you don't mind my asking, how long were you two married?"

"Three hellish years. We met in Houston," replied the woman, who seemed eager to talk. "Dick took over as manager of the restaurant where I worked. In the beginning, he was as charming as could be . . . so attentive and polite. I thought he was one of the nicest men I'd ever had the pleasure of knowing. I was a widow and he began courting me. When he proposed marriage, I immediately accepted, but I didn't take the name Wolf. I didn't like the sound of it. Then, not long after we moved in together, all hell broke loose. He began complaining and criticizing everything I did or didn't do. Night and day, he just kept yelling at me. He never hit me, but he sure threatened to . . . many times. I became very scared. At first, I foolishly thought everything was my fault and tried to make changes, but, eventually, I realized this man had a very different side to his personality. Then, one day, out of the blue, he told me we were moving. He said he'd always wanted to own his own business and was buying a restaurant that was for sale in Sunshine Valley, Arizona . . . the Crazy Cactus. I thought, maybe if he did this, it would make him happy and he'd return to being the sweet man I first met. Boy, was I wrong. I did everything I could to help him and even worked in the restaurant for a while. But, after almost two years of continual abuse, I decided I'd had enough. So, I finally found the courage to tell Dick that I wanted a divorce. He immediately agreed and said he'd been thinking the same thing."

"That's quite a story. Did you get a divorce?" asked Eve, even though she'd been told by Adam that it was pending.

"We started the process, but Dick was killed before everything became finalized. I must say, that was an incredibly lucky break for me. He told me he was going to leave me the house . . . just the house, nothing else. Now, because he died before the divorce went through and I'm the next of kin, I've inherited both the house and the restaurant, as well as all his money. He didn't have any living relatives and never made a will. I don't think he thought he was ever going to die."

"Now that you're the owner, does that mean you're going to continue running the restaurant, or do you plan to sell it?" asked Eve.

"No way do I want to sell it. It will stay open, but I plan to change the name. I'd like something a little more cheerful, but, so far, I don't have any ideas. I'm thinking all the time and I'm sure a nice name will come to me, sooner or later. I love the restaurant business and, based on my experience in Houston, I'm sure I can handle it. Donna is also going to help me," she said with a smile, as she pointed to the woman who was seated beside her. "I know the two of us will be able to manage it without difficulty."

"Yes, I'm really looking forward to it," replied the younger woman.

"Donna and I met shortly after Dick and I were married and we've become very close over the past three years. She's been living in Tucson, but is going to move in with me here in Sunshine Valley. The house is certainly big enough to comfortably accommodate two people."

"I never saw much of Dick Wolf and never knew him personally," continued Donna. "He wasn't my biological father. That man died in a car accident, just after I was born. Dick met and married my mother, when I was just a baby. I was only two years old when she died and he went away. I'm sure he didn't want to have the responsibility of caring for a small child. I was adopted by one of my aunts and grew up in Houston. When I was older and met Valerie, we immediately bonded. She was so kind to me and I now consider her to be my surrogate mother."

"I never had any children of my own," added Valerie, "so, I think of Donna as my surrogate daughter, even though I never knew her as a child. Now, we have such fun together and I know the two of us are going to enjoy running the restaurant together."

"This is fascinating," replied Eve, "but, where are my manners? I've been so intrigued by what you've been telling me, I forgot to ask if either of you would like something to drink. Water? A soft drink?"

"Well, maybe a glass of water. I've been talking so much, I'm a little thirsty," replied Valerie.

"Make that two," added Donna. "I'm getting thirsty just listening."

"I'll be right back." Eve pushed herself out of the chair, went into the house, and returned a few minutes later, carrying a tray with three tall glasses of water and a bowl of nuts.

As she looked at Valerie, Eve was suddenly reminded of the conversation she'd had with Peggy Walsh at the pool. She remembered that Peggy had said she'd seen a woman leaving Dick Wolf's office and this woman seemed to fit her description . . . short, grayish hair, glasses, nondescript clothes. I wonder. "If you don't mind, I have a question," she asked. "By any chance . . . did you happen to go to the restaurant the day your husband died?"

"How did you know that?" asked a surprised Valerie.

"Just a lucky guess."

"Yes, I was there, but I didn't kill him," continued the older woman.

"I certainly didn't mean to imply that you did. It's just that I've met so many people who were there that day," replied Eve in a noncommittal tone.

"I went to the office to bring something to Dick. After we decided to get a divorce, he didn't want to live with me any longer and he moved out of the house. He took all his belongings, but, apparently forgot a small black box that he kept in his closet. He called me and asked me, or, I should say, he told me, to bring it to him. He said he never wanted to set foot in that house again. Even though I didn't particularly want to go to the restaurant, I did as he asked and delivered the box to him. I was only in his office for a few minutes and, I assure you, he was his usual nasty self, but very much alive, when I left him."

"Have you spoken with the sheriff?" Eve asked reluctantly.

"Oh, yes. Well, not the sheriff himself, but, two of his officers came to my house and asked me questions. They were there for quite a while. I told them pretty much what I just told you, but I don't think they were very impressed. At one point, I noticed one of the officers had to stifle a yawn. They asked me what I wanted to do with Dick's body and I told them I'd pay for his cremation . . . that's all. There won't be a funeral or any burial . . . no public event. I'll just pay to have someone scatter his ashes in the desert . . . as far away from here as possible. When the officers were finished, they thanked me and told me not to leave town. They said they might have further questions. Leave town?. No way do I plan to leave town. I'm going to open a restaurant."

"Do you have any idea when you will re-open?" asked Eve.

"It won't be too long. I think it will just take a few weeks. I need a little more time to get some legal matters and paperwork straightened out," Valerie replied. "I want to make a few minor changes to the decor. I also want to try and get rid of anything that reminds me of Dick, especially in the office. Since we're also going to re-name the restaurant, I'll need a different sign as well, and I'll have to get some new menus printed."

"You know," began Eve, "based on what you just told me and everything else I've heard about your ex-husband, I'm surprised that the restaurant was so successful. People really seem to love it and, even though I haven't eaten there, I hear it's usually quite crowded."

"Yes, it's very popular," agreed Valerie. "That's due to the excellent food and service Dick provided. He always wanted the best and was very strict with the staff, the reason being money. He felt that the more customers he could draw in, the more money he'd earn . . . and, I must say, he did very well in that area. I hope to continue providing the best and Donna intends to help me achieve that goal. I'm going to make her my partner. She'll be co-owner. I think she deserves that," she said, with a smile.

"This may not be a proper question at this point, but I feel I need to ask it. By any chance, do you happen to know George Gomez?" Eve asked, haltingly.

"George? Of course, I know him . . . wonderful man," replied Valerie.

"I agree," said Eve, with a smile. "I'm so glad you think so too. I've met and spoken with him. He seems very nice and I feel sorry for all he's going through."

"So do I, and, as a matter of fact, I called him and we had a long talk. I told him that, once the restaurant re-opens, I want him to come back. He was thrilled and so am I. George was one of Dick's best employees and then, he had to go and fire him."

"Oh, Valerie," said Eve, as she leaned towards the woman. "Thank you. What a relief! I've been so concerned about him. This is wonderful news."

"Yes," replied Valerie. "I'm sure the restaurant will be a great success, especially since I'll have the help of both George and Donna. Right now, Donna is taking a course in Tucson at the university that focuses on the pioneering women of Arizona. It will be ending soon and when it does, she'll move here permanently."

"Pioneering women . . . that sounds fascinating," remarked Eve, as she edged closer to the two women.

"It is," replied Donna. "So much of the history of the West has been forgotten, especially when it comes to women. I've learned a great deal about their accomplishments. Throughout the nineteenth century and, even well into the twentieth century, the role of women was expected to be one of domestic provider and caregiver. They were expected to stay in the home and were certainly not encouraged to go out and start a business. Nevertheless, many women did, either out of necessity, or driven by their own inner desire. Quite a few of the women who came to Arizona in the nineteenth century, and later, started and managed hotels and restaurants . . . even mines. Women of all races and nationalities became entrepreneurs and some of them even accumulated great wealth, as a result of their efforts. And then, of course, because, in those days, the West was pretty much ruled by the gun, we even had our share of female outlaws. I'm afraid their names are more well known than those of the entrepreneurs . . . Annie Oakley, Calamity Jane, Belle Starr, and a few others."

"As far as I'm concerned, I plan to follow in the tradition of the entrepreneurs," said Valerie, with a laugh. "I'll leave the gun slinging to someone else."

"Good idea," replied Eve. "I think it's a little safer. You know, I've often thought about the early settlers who came across the country in covered wagons. I can't imagine what it must have been like. I wonder how people today would fare, if they had to make such a strenuous journey. We're all so spoiled these days, with our computers, iPads, cell phones, cars, etcetera. A hundred years ago, there was little water and food, no gas or electricity. I can't imagine what the summers must have been like with no electricity and, especially, no air-conditioning. It's mind boggling."

Donna leaned over towards Eve, eager to talk about her plans. "When I move here, I plan to do research on the pioneering women of Sunshine Valley and the surrounding area. I know there are a few distant relatives of some of the early women who live here now. I'm going to try to locate as many of them as possible. I want to see if they have any stories or photographs that they might be willing to share. I find that doing research is like being a detective . . . difficult, but also a lot of fun. I hope to write an article, or even a book, based on my research. I can't wait to get started."

"I want to read whatever you write," replied Eve. "I'd love to learn more about the early women of Sunshine Valley, and it sounds as if you already know quite a bit of history."

"I'll be sure to let you see the results of my current passion. I love sharing what I discover with others," added Donna, with a smile.

"I really admire writers," said Eve. "You need a good deal of patience. I know. I did quite a bit of writing when I was teaching. It usually takes a long time to see the outcome of all one's work. That's why I now prefer painting. The results of my efforts are much more immediate and I can make quick changes, if I don't like what I see."

Suddenly, Coco sprang to her feet and ran over to the front patio gate. Eve looked up and saw Adam, who was returning from the gym. "Well, Mr. Atlas, how did it go?" she asked.

"Great. I wish I'd joined the gym sooner. It's going to be a regular activity," replied her husband. "I jogged five miles, lifted a hundred pounds, and bicycled twenty miles. It's much more fun than just doing pushups."

"Good for you," replied Eve. "Now, come over here. I want you to meet Dick Wolf's widow, Valerie Wallace and her surrogate daughter, Donna Bates."

After the customary polite introductions, Valerie looked at Adam and began to speak. "I'm so glad you're here too. As I told your wife, I want to thank you both for finding my ex-husband's body."

Adam listened carefully, as the woman briefly recounted everything she'd just told Eve.

"Well, I'm glad things are working out for both of you and I certainly look forward to dining in your restaurant. Now, if you will excuse me, I need to take a shower and put on some decent clothes. And, thank you for stopping by. I know we'll be seeing each other again shortly," said Adam, as he smiled at the two women, then turned and went into the house.

"I was hoping your husband would be here. I'll let you know when the restaurant is ready to re-open. I want you both to be my guests for dinner. Now, I see you've got your easel set up and I'm sure you're eager to get back to your painting. You've been so kind to listen to my ranting and we have taken up enough of your time. We can talk more at a later date."

"Before you go, I want to let you know about an art exhibit I'm having at the Sunshine Gallery," said Eve, as she escorted the two women to the gate. "If you're interested, there will be a reception on Saturday, April seventh, from two to five, in the afternoon. You're not obligated to buy anything. You can just look around and, hopefully, enjoy my work."

"Of course, we're interested and would love to see what you've done," replied Valerie. "We both love art and we'll be sure to be there. You can count on it." The two women exited and returned to their car.

After a few minutes, a clean and well-groomed Adam emerged from the house. "They seem nice," he said to Eve.

"Yes, I liked both of them, but, I wonder . . ." began Eve, but Adam didn't let her finish her thought.

"Don't tell me . . . I'm afraid to ask," he said, somewhat reluctantly.

"You heard what she said. She hated her husband and she certainly benefited from his death. She didn't express any concern over the fact that his killer is still out there. Actually, if you think about it, Valerie Wallace probably had the strongest motive of anybody to kill. This is turning into a real puzzle . . ."

Once again, Adam didn't let his wife finish her thought. "No more. Why don't you just stick to your crossword puzzles? They're much safer. I don't want to hear anything more that has to do with Dick Wolf. I didn't hear a word about him and the murder, when I was at the gym and that's the way I like it. Now, let's just have a bite to eat before we go over to Doty and Paula's house."

"Oh, dear," gasped Eve. "I forgot all about that. When do they want us to come over? Do we need to bring anything?"

"We still have a couple of hours and no, Doty said it will be very simple . . . just a few appetizers and they have everything they need. She said that Frank is going to give a little piano concert and thought we'd enjoy hearing him play."

"Wonderful," replied Eve. "It's always simple at their house and it will be refreshing to just sit back and listen to some lovely music, and not talk about murder. I know that Coco is always welcome, but I think we better leave her at home, this time. If she hears the music, I'm afraid she'll start to sing along."

After finishing their lunch, Eve turned to Adam and asked, "Do you think what I'm wearing is okay? I really don't feel like changing clothes and Doty and Paula are usually pretty casual."

"What? I thought you might want to wear an evening gown," chided Adam. "We are going to a concert, after all."

"I'm afraid all my gowns are at the cleaners," replied Eve, with a laugh.

"And my tux is getting a bit tight. I guess they'll just have to take us the way we are," added Adam.

After a short rest, the couple left the house and headed down the street. As they walked, Eve began reviewing in her mind everything that Valerie had told her. Once again, she had a distant look on her face that her husband had come to recognize so well. "Yes . . . now, what is it that's running through that complex head of yours?" he asked, in a friendly voice.

"I'm so happy for George Gomez," said Eve. "Valerie really seems to appreciate him. Being re-hired will make such a difference for him and his family."

"Yes, even if he did kill her husband, I don't think it matters to her. She's probably grateful. Maybe the job is a reward," replied Adam.

"He didn't kill Dick Wolf," snapped Eve. "I'm sure of it and you told me the sheriff's men found no evidence to indicate that he did do it. So, just leave it at that. Eventually . . . hopefully . . . the real killer will be found. I'm just concerned that it might take too long."

When Adam and Eve arrived at the front door to Doty and Paula's house, they didn't have to knock or ring the bell. It was wide open and they walked right in.

"Hello, everyone," said Adam. His greeting was followed by a chorus of welcomes from Doty, Paula, Jackie, and Frank, who was seated by the piano.

"Come in and sit down," said Doty, as she waved them into the living room. "You're in for a real treat."

Eve looked around and noticed that everyone was dressed very simply, except for Jackie, who was wearing the same bright red dress she wore to the barbecue.

She obviously loves that dress, thought Eve, and felt that, this time, she should offer a compliment. "I love your dress," she said. "The color is so becoming to you."

"Thank you," replied Jackie. "This is my lucky dress. I feel good when I wear it and it's brought me a great deal of happiness."

"Before I forget it," said Adam, as he addressed the group, "you probably already know about Eve's art show and reception on the seventh. I hope to see everyone there."

"We're becoming so cultured," said Paula, "art exhibits and piano concerts. I wonder what we'll do next . . . and, yes, we're all planning on attending the reception. We're looking forward to it."

"Well, before we get started, I want to report some wonderful news," said Jackie, as she looked at Adam and Eve.

"Tell us," Eve urged. "What is it?"

"I'm so excited. It's hard for me to even talk," replied Jackie, as she gasped for air.

"Calm down and take a deep breath," said Eve.

"I'm going to Alaska," the woman blurted out.

Eve looked at Adam and smiled, as she recalled what he'd told her.

"Frank has asked me to go on a seven-day cruise with him to Alaska. The ship leaves from Seattle and goes up the coast, making stops at several ports, both in Canada and Alaska. I'm really thrilled. I've never done much traveling . . . a couple of short trips to Minnesota and in Wisconsin with my family, when I was little. The only boat I've ever been on was to Mackinac Island. We'll see glaciers, migrating whales, and beautiful landscapes . . . I'm so excited. We'll be leaving in a few weeks. It's a good thing I brought some of my winter clothes with me when I left Milwaukee. I must have known that I'd need them some day, but I never thought it would be in Alaska," she said, with a laugh.

"That sounds like a fun trip," said Adam. "I've never been on it, myself, but I have friends who've taken that cruise and they just loved it. I'm sure you'll have a wonderful time."

"That sounds very exciting," added Eve. "How will you get to Seattle?"

"We're going to fly there from Tucson, then catch the boat," replied Jackie.

"I envy you," said Paula. "You're lucky you don't get seasick. When we were in California, a few years ago, Doty and I once took a boat cruise to Catalina Island and I was nauseated for the entire trip. I didn't get to see or enjoy anything. I wouldn't go near a boat again and, now that I live in the desert, that's one worry I can put out of my mind."

Turning to Eve, Jackie exclaimed with enthusiasm, "I'll be sure to take my camera with me. Maybe I'll be able to capture some beautiful scenes that will inspire you."

"Great," replied Eve. "I don't know if I'll be able to paint them, but I definitely would like to see your pictures."

As everyone settled back, Eve began looking around the sparsely furnished room. She noticed a blank wall above the fireplace and thought one of her paintings would fit in perfectly. She decided that she would give Doty and Paula one of her early Georgia O'Keeffe inspirations. *It's the least I can do*, she reflected, *since they've been so kind to me and Adam and the colors in the painting would really liven up the room.*

"Okay, everybody. Let's have some appetizers," said Doty, as she began passing around a tray. "You can now relax, sit back, and listen to a lovely piano concert performed by Sunshine Valley's one and only Frank Howell."

"Thank you," replied a smiling Frank, as he turned to face his audience. "First, I'm going to play a Ravel waltz, followed by some Schubert songs, then a little Debussy, and I'll end with a Beethoven sonata that I'm sure you'll all recognize. I hope you enjoy." He adjusted the bench and slowly began to play.

Eve was amazed at both Frank's musical ability and how he was able to turn the pages of the sheet music with such ease. Once he finished his last piece, everyone began clapping. "That was fabulous," exclaimed Jackie. "You're brilliant. You could go on the stage."

"Thank you, thank you," said Frank. "Now, would anyone else like to play? Doty, I know how talented you are. How about it?"

"Not today. Besides, you're much too difficult an act to follow."

"We always love listening to Frank play," remarked Paula. "He's so gifted. I can't wait 'til Christmas. We'll all get together and sing carols to his accompaniment."

After consuming a few more appetizers, Eve looked over at Adam and gave him the familiar nod that meant it was time to leave.

"This has been truly enjoyable," said Adam, as he rose from his chair. "You have quite a talent, Frank, and, I must say, I'm a little jealous of you."

"That makes us even," replied Frank, with a grin.

"I'm sorry we have to leave, but Coco has been alone too long," said Eve.

"Oh, you should have brought her with you," exclaimed Jackie.

"We usually do bring her, but, this time, I'm afraid she would have started howling when she heard the music . . . her way of singing," Eve explained.

On their way home, Eve turned to Adam and began to speak. "I didn't know Frank was such an accomplished pianist and I don't think I've ever seen him this happy. He used to be so shy and retiring when Olive was alive. Now, he seems like a different person."

"You're right," responded Adam. "His new found freedom has really had a positive effect. I'm very happy for him."

As they continued walking, Eve became more serious. "I know I shouldn't be thinking about Dick Wolf, but I can't seem to help myself. I understand that this was to be a piano concert, but I didn't get the impression that anyone was particularly concerned that a killer might be on the loose in Sunshine Valley. The reaction of most people appears to be just the opposite. I think Dick Wolf's death has brought a good deal of joy to so many folks . . . the restaurant employees, his wife, his daughter, Jack Slater. Both those who knew him, as well as others who didn't know him, seem happy or unconcerned that he's dead. Also, I didn't even get the impression that Sheriff Warner was particularly upset when he came to the restaurant."

"I suppose, after all the complaints he got from folks, he was surprised that somebody didn't kill the man sooner," responded Adam. Eager to change the subject of Dick Wolf, he continued speaking. "I believe part of Frank's positive change is also due to the arrival of Jackie. I think she's very good for him and now that they're going on a cruise together, they'll undoubtedly become closer."

"I'm sure you're right," responded Eve. "They really seem to hit it off and, of course, the cruise will give them the opportunity to get to know each other better. By the way, I'm curious. Why do you think Frank is jealous of you?"

"Because I have a beautiful and talented wife," replied Adam, without hesitation.

"Of course," laughed Eve, "I'm sorry I asked. I should have known."

As usual, Adam and Eve heard Coco begin barking as they approached the house.

"Come on, little girl," said Adam, as he turned the key and opened the door. "I know you've been waiting for us. It's time for your walk." He put on the dog's leash and went out again.

When he returned, Adam looked at Eve and began to speak with enthusiasm. "You know, as I told you, I really enjoyed the gym and I was wondering if we should buy an exercycle. The patio is a perfect place for it and both of us could use it."

"How about buying some real bicycles? I see quite a few people riding by me when I go to the pool," replied Eve.

"We could get both . . . an exercycle for the home and bicycles for outside. What do you think?"

"I'm all for that," agreed Eve. "I don't want to give up my exercise at the pool, but I also think bicycling would be fun, and, since I sit for so many hours at my easel, it would be good to get up once in a while and use an exercycle."

"Isn't paradise wonderful? Nice weather, beautiful scenery, good friends, good food, culture, exercise . . ."

"And murder," added Eve.

"Okay, Deputy Sheriff Eve Iverson, enough. Let's watch a little television before we retire . . . I mean, go to bed." They both laughed, as they walked into the den and made themselves comfortable.

Chapter 6

Once the day of the reception at the art gallery arrived, Eve was all keyed up. Although she'd rehearsed in her mind answers to the many possible questions she thought people would ask her, she was still concerned that she might have missed something.

As they were preparing to leave the house, Adam sensed his wife's anxiety and attempted to provide some encouragement. "Try not to worry so much. I think you're going to be a real success. I just saw a notice in the *Sunshine Valley Times* about the show. I'm sure it will draw a lot of art lovers . . . not just our friends, but tourists and residents, as well. You want to bet you sell a few paintings?"

"That would be great, but, for now, I just want to get through this event. You better stay close to me," replied Eve, nervously. "I'm really not sure what to expect and I might need to rely on you for support."

"Even though I'm not the artist, I'll do what I can, if there are any problems," Adam assured his wife. "But, you'll be fine. I'd say that most people who go to an art show aren't aggressive and won't give you a hard time. I think they're usually pretty supportive. I'm quite sure you won't have any difficulty with their questions or comments."

"Do you like the outfit I'm wearing?" Eve asked, as she ran her hands down the front of her light blue silk blouse and pants. "I think it looks sort of artistic."

"It's perfect and goes very well with your blond hair. You look beautiful. All you need now is a beret," replied Adam, with a smile.

"That's a cliché," snapped Eve. "Come on, let's go and get this over with."

Although several cars were parked in front of the gallery, Adam managed to find the last empty space. "Look," he said, as he pointed out the window. "There's a sign about your exhibit. It has your name on it and even a reproduction of one of your paintings."

"That's nice, but I still feel a bit queasy," said Eve, flatly. "I love the idea that my paintings are on display, but I'm mostly scared."

"You needn't be. I know there are a lot of people who admire what you're doing and I'm one of them," replied Adam, as he put his arm around his wife's shoulder.

Once inside, the Iversons were greeted by Jack Slater. "Good. You're a little early. Folks should be arriving soon. Now, tell me what you think," he said, waving his arm.

The gallery included one large main room and a smaller one off to the side. Eve made a quick scan of the walls and her canvases, and was pleased with what she saw. "I love the frames. You were right. They really enhance the paintings."

"They're small," replied Jack, "but, they do the trick. They help the viewer focus. When a canvas is sold, the buyer can always replace the frame with a different one, if he or she chooses."

"I love what you've done and I wouldn't change anything," remarked Adam.

"Come here, you two," continued Jack. "I want you both to see what I had printed." As he led the couple back to the front door, he pointed to a stack of postcards that were neatly piled up on a little table.

"My goodness," gasped Eve, "these are about me and they even have a color photo of one of my paintings on them. They're beautiful. You've really outdone yourself."

"Not at all . . . take a few with you and give them to your friends. When people come in, they can pick one up. I think we might have a big crowd. My mailing list is quite large and I've sent out quite a few notices about your exhibit and today's reception."

As Eve picked up a handful of cards and put them in her purse, Jack's nephew, Tommy, emerged from the back office and greeted the Iversons. Today, like his uncle, he was dressed in a Western outfit from head to toe. Eve noticed that he even had an empty holster buckled around his waist.

"It looks like you're in good company," she said to Adam, who was wearing his favorite Western garb, including a broad-brimmed Stetson hat. "At least you're not toting a gun. I don't want any guns at my exhibit, toy, or otherwise."

Suddenly, the gallery door opened and in walked a smiling Doty, Paula, and Jackie. "Hi everyone," chirped Doty. "We thought we'd come early, before the crowds arrive. Frank dropped us off and is parking the car. He'll be joining us in a few minutes."

"Well, we're off to a good start . . . now that the three musketeers have arrived," replied Eve, cheerfully. She brought Jack over to her friends and introduced them, thinking it best not to make any jokes about Jack and Jackie's names.

As Paula seated herself in an armchair near the door, Doty and Jackie began walking through the gallery and looking at the paintings. To Eve's surprise, she heard Doty voice quite a few astute comments, as she passed each one.

"Doty seems to know a lot about art," Eve said to Paula.

"Yes," replied the woman. "She took quite a few art classes when she was younger. She's always had a secret desire to become a painter, but she doesn't talk about it much, because she hasn't produced anything . . . at least, not yet."

"Why not?" asked Eve.

"As you well know, supplies, and especially canvases, can be very expensive," Paula replied, hesitantly. "However, she's done some pencil sketches of me and Frank. They're really excellent. I'll have to show them to you, the next time you come over. I think you're in for a nice surprise."

"I'd love to see what she's done," replied Eve. "I never knew she was talented in that way." She turned when she heard the door open and saw Frank.

"The spaces are really filling up out there," he said, as he entered the gallery.

"Oh, Frank . . . come over here," called Jackie, from across the room. "I want your opinion. What do you think? Do you like this one?"

Both Adam and Frank joined Jackie, who was standing in front of a multi-colored desert landscape.

"I love it . . . great colors and shapes," replied Frank. Adam nodded in agreement.

"I think what you've done is fabulous. If I had enough money, I'd buy all of them," Jackie said to Eve, who slowly approached her, "but, today, I think this is the one I'm going to get. Yes . . . definitely. I want to buy this one. I have the perfect place for it in my house."

"Oh, Jackie, do you mean it?" Eve was caught off guard by Jackie's surprise offer. It wasn't something she could have anticipated.

"Let me find Jack. I want to let him know that I'm going to buy this painting before someone else grabs it."

"I'm right behind you," replied Jack, who'd been listening intently to the conversation. "If you're serious, please come into my office and we'll do the paperwork." Both Jackie and Frank followed him to the back of the gallery.

After a few minutes, Jack returned and placed a "Sold" sign next to Eve's painting. "There," he said, with a smile, "one down and nineteen to go."

"How about that," said Eve, as she looked intently at her husband. "I can't believe it. I just made my first sale."

"You deserve it," Jack replied. "I can assure you, this is just the beginning. I'm quite certain there will also be a few more sales before the day is over. Your work is very appealing."

At two o'clock exactly, the front door opened and people began streaming in. It didn't take long before the gallery filled up. Eve recognized a few faces from the pool, but others were new to her. She walked around slowly and introduced herself. She was very pleased that she'd rehearsed so well and was able to answer all the questions that were thrown at her. Looking through the crowd, she happened to notice Dick Wolf's widow, Valerie Wallace and her surrogate daughter, Donna.

"Valerie," said Eve, as she weaved her way towards the two women. "I didn't see you two come in. I can't believe all the people we've attracted . . . and so early. I'm glad you were both able to make it."

"We didn't want to miss your exhibit. I've been looking at your work and I think you really have a beautiful gift. Just to let you know, I'm going to buy three of your paintings. Not only do I admire your work, but, I want to make up for what Dick did . . . "

She broke off and held up her hand, as Eve started to protest. "Don't say a word yet. I think your paintings will fit in very nicely in the restaurant. We have a banquet room . . . I don't know if you ever saw it, but there's not much hanging on the walls now. Your paintings will really be a nice addition to the room. I've already spoken to the gallery owner and showed him the paintings I want. It's a done deal, so, don't try to stop me now."

"Oh, Valerie . . . I'm really flattered and don't quite know what to say, except to thank you," Eve answered, haltingly.

As they were conversing, Tommy emerged from the back office and posted "Sold" signs next to another three paintings. "At this rate, we may not have anything left by the end of the day," he said, as he winked at Eve. "You'll have to go home and quickly do some more."

"Don't worry. I'm really inspired," replied Eve, with a big smile.

"Well," said Valerie, we're going to make our exit now. Donna and I have quite a bit of work ahead of us. But, I'm wondering . . . if you're free tomorrow, do you think you could come by the restaurant? I want to show you some of the changes we've made and get your artistic opinion about a few things."

"So far, I'm quite free," replied Eve. "I don't know if I'll be of much help, but I'll give it my best effort. What time would you like me to come by?"

"I think around one o'clock would be good."

"See you tomorrow . . . and thank you so much for today," said Eve, as she slowly escorted the two women to the door.

Turning around, Eve saw Doty, Jackie, and Frank walking towards her. "This is really a wonderful exhibit and we love your work, but, we're going to leave now and make room for the serious buyers," said Doty.

"Come on Paula. We can wait outside, while Frank goes for the car." The older woman raised herself slowly and joined her two friends.

"Just a second," said Eve, with a smile, as she reached out her hand to Jackie. "I'm so glad you like my work and I want to thank you for helping to make my day a success. It was very nice of you to buy one of my paintings."

"You'll have to come over and see where I hang it," replied Jackie, who was also smiling.

Turning to Doty, Eve asked, "By the way, are you and Paula going to be home later this evening? I have a little something for you that I'd like to drop off when I'm finished here."

"Well, if we don't go dancing, I think we'll be home," replied Doty. "Feel free, but, just to let you know, we usually go to bed around nine."

"I'll be leaving here around five o'clock and will try to come over as early as I can. I certainly wouldn't want to disturb your sleep."

After escorting her friends to the door, Eve turned and, once again, began weaving her way through the crowd that kept growing. For the most part, both men and women talked about her art work and she answered their questions without difficulty. She was thankful that she was able to hold her own and not have to rely on Adam. Over the humming of voices, she thought she heard someone mention Dick Wolf's name, but couldn't tell where it was coming from. "That's the way we deal with tyrants here in the wild west, we off 'em," said the man with a hoarse laugh.

Although Eve didn't want to discuss anything related to the murder, to her dismay, this was a topic of interest to many of the people who began coming into the gallery and approaching her.

"So, you're Deputy Sheriff Eve Iverson," said one man in a gruff voice, as he pushed his way in her direction.

"That's Honorary Deputy Sheriff and it's not something I'm prepared to discuss," replied Eve, curtly. She had difficulty controlling her anger whenever someone asked her questions about Dick Wolf that she wasn't prepared for, or inclined to answer. On and on, one inane question after another was hurled at her:

"What did the body look like?"

"How did you happen to find the body?"

"How well did you know Dick Wolf?"

"Who do you think killed him?"

"Do you think George Gomez did it?"

"How is Dick Wolf's wife handling her husband's death?"

"Do you think his wife killed him?"

"What's the sheriff doing to find the killer?"

"Will you ever go to that restaurant again?"

As her annoyance escalated, Eve tried to avoid responding and wondered if most of the people who were now coming into the gallery were there to confront her about the murder, rather than to look at the paintings. As she glanced across the crowded room, she noticed that a small group of men had gathered around Adam in a far corner. She feared that he was also being deluged with similar questions.

After a couple of hours of discussing her work with the genuine art enthusiasts and managing her best to avoid the people who were just interested in gossip, Eve noticed Tommy and a woman walk over to two of her paintings and post "Sold" signs. She immediately joined them.

"Looking around at all these canvases, I've become a big fan of your work," said the woman, as she smiled at Eve. "I'm having these two shipped back to Chicago with me. I can't wait to show them to some of my art loving friends."

"How kind of you," replied Eve, as she shook the woman's hand.

"Not at all," continued the woman. "I come to Sunshine Valley every winter and enjoy going to all the art galleries between here and Nogales. I have to say, without a doubt, your work is the best that I've seen."

"What a wonderful compliment, and, now, my paintings are going to be traveling across the country, because of you. I'm very flattered." Eve was beaming, as she turned and walked over to Adam, who'd managed to extricate himself from the group that had cornered him. They were immediately joined by Jack Slater.

"You can be proud of yourself," said Jack, his eyes glowing, as he looked at Eve. "This reception has been a big success. I had a feeling you would do well and I was right. We're on quite a roll. You sold six paintings in one afternoon. I wouldn't be surprised if you sell a few more before the end of the exhibit."

"Yes, I can't get over it. It's more than I'd expected. It certainly makes me want to continue painting," replied Eve.

By five o'clock, the gallery had thinned out considerably. When the last man made his way to the front door, he turned and waved at Adam and Eve. "Good-bye, deputies, nice meeting you both," he said, then exited.

"Phew," sighed Eve. "This has been a real workout."

"You're doing great," said Jack. "I will definitely be in touch with you and I expect to have a large check for you in a few days."

Eve looked around the gallery one more time, then grabbed Adam's arm. "Let's go. I've had enough for today."

As they were driving home, Adam was the first to speak. "That was quite a turnout, but, I'm almost afraid to ask . . . how did you like your first artist reception?"

"Well, overall, I would say it was both good and bad," replied Eve, with some reluctance.

"What do you mean? You sold six paintings . . . that's good, isn't it?" Adam was somewhat surprised by his wife's mixed reaction.

"That's the good part. I also received quite a few compliments about my work, for which I'm greatly appreciative," replied Eve.

"And the bad part?" asked Adam.

"I can't believe all the talk about Dick Wolf that I heard. I think at least half of the people who came to the exhibit were only interested in hearing about his murder. I had to fend off so many questions. I'm sure I annoyed a lot of folks, but, I just couldn't bring myself to deal with that subject. And you? I think you had your share of busybodies, as well."

"I sure did. I wasn't up to talking about the murder, either. I tried to be as brief and tactful as possible, when someone approached me. One fellow even jokingly suggested that you and I might be the culprits, but, I just ignored him," replied Adam.

"No way . . . I don't understand why so many people are interested in Dick Wolf's death. Don't they have anything better to do with their time?"

"That's the problem," said Adam. "They have too much time on their hands with nothing to do . . . and a murder gives them something to dwell on and gossip about."

"Maybe I'm just a bit too keyed up, but, at one point, I even wondered if the killer was at the gallery," sighed Eve.

"Don't . . . this day is supposed to be about art . . . not about murder," chided Adam.

"True. That's what you should have told the curiosity seekers. Anyway, there were enough people at the gallery who came specifically to see my paintings and, you were right, nobody asked me anything that I wasn't able to answer. I'm going to focus on the good part and forget the rest."

"You took the words out of my mouth," replied Adam, with a smile.

After a few silent moments, Eve continued to speak. "It was so nice of Valerie to buy three paintings and I'm really surprised that Jackie wanted one, as well. She must not have any money worries."

"Between you and me," replied Adam, "I think Frank paid for the painting."

"Really? I should have guessed. He seems to be quite comfortable, these days. I think Olive must have left him a tidy sum." After a short pause, Eve continued speaking. "You know, I didn't see Peggy Walsh. She told me she'd be coming to the exhibit. Maybe it was just too crowded and I missed her. I'll find out when I see her at the pool."

As they were driving, the car lurched when Adam tried to avoid hitting a roadrunner that was crossing in front of them. "Good reason for seat belts. Are you okay?" he asked Eve.

"Yes, I'm fine. I saw it coming. By the way, I told Doty and Paula that we'd stop by their place after the reception. I want to give them one of my paintings."

"That's very generous of you," responded Adam.

"Well, they've been very good to us and they don't have much money. The last time we were at their house, I noticed a bare space on the wall in the living room, above the fire place. I think one of my early paintings would fit in perfectly. Let's stop at home and get the canvas, then drive over to their place, before it gets much later. I'm anxious to see how it looks in their home."

"I'll hang it up for them," said Adam. "I have just the right tools in the shed."

"Great. I think they're in for a nice surprise. I didn't tell them why we were coming, just that I had something for them."

Eve was delighted at the prospect of giving one of her paintings to Doty and Paula and hoped they would like it. When they pulled into their driveway, they quickly entered the house and went out to the shed on the patio. Eve showed Adam the painting in question. He picked it up, together with his tools, then headed back to the car.

"I think we need to take Coco with us," said Eve. "She's been alone too long." At the sound of her name, the dog began barking, as Eve put on her leash.

After a short two-minute drive, the Iversons arrived at their neighbors' house and were greeted by Doty. "What's this?" she asked with surprise, as she noticed Adam carrying a canvas.

"I told you I had something for you," said Eve, with a smile. "I brought one of my paintings for you. I thought it would fit in nicely in your living room."

Once inside, Adam turned the canvas and revealed Eve's painting, which depicted several colorful desert flowers.

"What? Are you serious? This is for us?" gasped Doty, as she regarded at the canvas. "Look, Paula. Look what Adam and Eve have brought us."

"It's beautiful," remarked Paula. "But, are you sure? I don't think we can afford it."

"Don't be silly. It's a gift. I thought it would look nice on that wall," replied Eve, as she pointed to the fireplace. "Adam can even hang it for you."

After much animated conversation, Adam took out his tools and hung the canvas where Eve indicated. "How's that? What do you think? Do you like it?" he asked the two women.

"It's fabulous," replied Doty and Paula in unison.

"The flowers are beautiful. I love the colors. It makes the room come alive," said Paula, thoughtfully.

"This is the nicest gift we've ever received," added Doty. "Thank you so much. You're too kind."

"Since she's become a successful and famous artist, Eve wants to be able to share her talent with friends she cares about," said Adam, as he smiled at Paula. "Even Coco seems to like it," he added, as the dog looked up at the wall and began wagging her tail.

"Now," said Paula, as she walked over to a table and opened the drawer, "I told you that Doty is also very artistic. I want to show you some of the pencil sketches that she's done. There's one of me and also one of Frank." She took out two sheets of white letterhead paper and handed them to Eve.

"Doty," exclaimed Eve, "who knew? You've been keeping this a secret. You're very talented. Look, Adam," she said, as she handed the drawings to her husband.

"Very impressive. You really captured their unique expressions," replied Adam.

"You have to do some more," said Eve, with encouragement. "I'd also love to see what you might create with a little paint and a canvas."

"Maybe . . . some day," answered Doty, with reluctance. "It's just that supplies are very expensive, as you well know."

After more discussion about art and Eve's painting, the Iversons excused themselves.

"This has been a very long day and I've been talking for hours," sighed Eve. "I'm tired of hearing my own voice and I think I need to go home and just be quiet."

"Yes," replied Paula. "You had quite a successful exhibit. I can't imagine what it must be like to have to interact with so many people and answer all their questions. I couldn't have managed such an ordeal. Go home now. Relax and don't talk any more . . . except maybe to say 'good night' to Adam . . . and, thank you so much for your precious gift. We are really going to enjoy it and you will too when you come here."

On their way home, Adam volunteered to make a light meal for the two of them.

"I could use something to eat," said Eve, "but, nothing too heavy. We have a few dinners in the freezer that would do the trick . . . or, better yet, just a simple salad."

Once inside, Adam and Eve both headed for the den. Eve threw herself on the couch and propped up her feet, as Adam walked over to the desk. "Looks like we have a phone message," he said.

"I hope it's nothing bad," sighed Eve.

Adam picked up the phone and listened to the message. "That was Jack and guess what? You sold another painting. He said someone came in after we left, looked around, liked what he saw, then bought one. So, that makes seven sales in one day."

"This is truly more than I expected. Maybe I should have started my art career when I was younger . . . forget teaching."

"Now that you're beginning to accumulate so much money, do you have any plans for how you're going to spend your newly acquired wealth? A yacht? A house in the mountains?" asked Adam, teasingly.

"As a matter of fact, I've been thinking about that very subject," replied Eve. "First, the exercycle, then a couple of bicycles, some more art supplies, and a new toy for Coco. I'd also like to give a little money to Doty for art supplies, so she can get started painting."

"That's quite a list . . . and, a very nice one," replied Adam.

"Weren't you going to make some dinner?" asked Eve with a yawn.

"I'm on my way." Adam saluted, exited the room, and went into the kitchen.

The remainder of the evening was quiet and, true to her promise, Eve hardly said a word. As they were getting into bed, Adam asked, "Which word game will it be tonight?"

"I'll let you know in the morning," replied his wife, with a yawn.

Except for a chorus of coyotes wailing in the distance, an all encompassing silence descended upon the desert.

Chapter 7

When they awakened the following morning, Adam turned to Eve and asked, "Well, I'm curious. You told me you'd let me know. What game did you play this time?"

"I didn't have to . . . I was so tired, I fell asleep as soon as I put my head on the pillow. Maybe standing and talking for several hours is the secret to a good night's sleep. And you? Were you able to tune out?"

"I had a little difficulty turning off the day's events, so I used one of your games to help clear my mind," replied Adam.

"Which one was that?" asked Eve.

"I went through the alphabet, from A to Z, and tried to think of cities in the United States."

"That's an easy one."

"Really? What about Q and X?"

Without hesitation, Eve responded, "How about Quincy, Illinois, and Xenia, Ohio?"

"Smarty pants," replied Adam, teasingly.

"I should never have told you that," said Eve, as she slowly rolled out of bed. "Well, it looks like another beautiful day in the desert," she continued, as she opened the drapes. "I just love the mornings here . . . bright sunshine, beautiful blue sky, and the shapes of the clouds are fabulous. We're so lucky to have found this little haven."

"Yes, we are. So, what's on your agenda for today?" asked Adam, as he stretched his arms, shook his legs, then managed to push himself up.

"First, it's the pool," replied Eve, with a yawn. "Later, I promised to go and see Valerie at the restaurant. She's made some changes and wants my opinion about a few things. After that, I'm free to do anything you like, but, I bet I know where you're headed this morning."

"Right you are . . . it's off to the gym. What time are you supposed to see Valerie?" asked Adam.

"She said one o'clock."

"That's good. I'll be home before then and you can have the car. Maybe that's another item you should put on your list . . . a second car," replied Adam, as he smiled at his wife.

"For now, I'll be satisfied with an exercycle. The Rolls will have to wait."

After finishing their morning routine, Eve was the first to leave the house. She slowly strolled down the street, humming parts of the Beethoven sonata that she'd heard Frank play on the piano. Upon entering the pool area, she spotted Peggy Walsh, who was sitting in her usual spot. She called to her, but the woman appeared deeply involved in conversation with a man who was seated beside her and didn't hear Eve's greeting.

Suddenly, the man pointed in Eve's direction and Peggy turned around. "Oh, Eve," she chirped. "I didn't see you coming. We were just talking about you. Come closer. I don't think you've met Arthur."

"No, I don't believe we've met," replied Eve, as she shook the man's hand, then pulled over an empty chair and seated herself beside Peggy.

"So, from what Arthur has been telling me, I understand you had a very successful reception yesterday," remarked Peggy.

"Yes, it was great. I looked for you, but, didn't see you anywhere. Did something happen? I thought you said you would be coming," Eve asked, cautiously.

"Actually, I started out to go there with two friends. We drove over to the gallery and had every intention of going in, but we couldn't find a parking space and then we saw a long line of people waiting to enter. So, we changed our plans and decided to get a bite to eat, instead. I thought the gallery would be much too hectic and I know that the show will be up for at least another week. But, I do want to see your work, so I plan on going again, when it's not so crowded."

"You're right. We had a lot of people. Even I had difficulty moving through the crowd, so it's probably just as well that you didn't try to come in," replied Eve.

"But, Arthur went to your show. That's what we were just talking about," added Peggy.

"Really? I'm afraid I didn't have a chance to speak with you," replied Eve, as she glanced over at the man. "Since you were there, you saw how many people we drew in."

"Arthur was telling me that, besides looking at your art work, a lot of folks were also curious to meet you and Adam and wanted to know more about your discovery of Dick Wolf's body," added Peggy.

"Yes, I'm afraid so. I was asked quite a few questions about that subject, but, I really didn't have much to say, nor did I want to. I didn't think it was the appropriate time or place to talk about murder. Besides, I was too focused on my paintings." Eve tried to sound as noncommittal as possible.

"From what I hear," began Arthur, "more and more people are starting to think that Dick Wolf's wife, Valerie, killed him and not George Gomez. It appears that she had the most to gain by his death . . . at least, financially. She inherited everything. I understand a divorce was in the works and hadn't yet been finalized. If he'd died a few days later, she wouldn't have seen a penny. One of my friends who works in the restaurant, knows Valerie and he saw her and a younger woman come in and walk to the back office on the morning of his murder. Who knows what happened next? But, I'll bet you something happened behind the door. She could easily have shot him."

Eve sat silently, as she listened to the man express his opinion. She thought he seemed much more interested in Dick Wolf's murder than in her art work and was probably part of the group that had surrounded Adam at the exhibit. When she felt that he'd finished, she turned to Peggy and began to speak. "Last time I was here, you told me that when you were in the restaurant, you saw a woman leaving Dick Wolf's office. Do you remember if she was she alone?"

"You know, I was a bit preoccupied and didn't pay that much attention," replied Peggy. "I just vaguely remember the woman I told you about. As far as I know, she was alone, but I wouldn't swear to it. There may have been some other people in the hallway, but I'm not sure. The restaurant was very busy. I never met Dick Wolf's wife, so I can't tell you if she was the woman I saw."

Eve pushed herself out of the chair and removed her robe. "Now," she said, as she inhaled deeply, "I'm going to do what I came here for. I really need a good swim." She walked over to the pool, climbed down the ladder, and began doing a few laps. Swimming always calmed her mind and she felt that's what she needed now. Even though there was a small crowd gathered around the pool, she was pleased that only one other person was in the water.

"You're doing great," Peggy called to her. "Keep it up."

After completing six laps, Eve swam back over to the ladder and slowly climbed out of the water. "I think that's enough for one day," she said, as she began to dry herself.

"I envy you folks who know how to swim," remarked Peggy. "Maybe one of these days, I'll give it a go. I need the exercise and I'm often tempted."

"You should try it," said Arthur, with encouragement. "If you like, I'll even hold you up so that you don't sink."

"Let me think about it," replied Peggy, with a laugh. Then, changing the subject, she turned to Eve. "I know there were a lot of people at your exhibit, but, how did it go? Did you sell any paintings?" she asked.

"Oh yes, I certainly did," replied Eve, as she continued drying herself. "It was a very successful reception and I sold several pieces. I think Jack and his nephew did a terrific job of getting the word out."

"Nephew . . . hah!" interjected Arthur. "That's what Jack calls him, but I doubt very much they're related," he said, disdainfully.

Eve thought she'd heard enough and put on her robe. She didn't like this man and had no desire to engage in any further conversation with him. Although it was a bit difficult, she tried to sound as cheerful as possible, as she prepared to leave. "Well, I have to be going, now... nice meeting you, Arthur, and I'll undoubtedly see you again. And, Peggy . . . I know, for sure, I'll see you again."

"I hope we didn't say anything to upset you," said Peggy, as she leaned forward.

"Of course not. It's just that I have to be somewhere in a little while," replied Eve, flatly. She had no intention of revealing that she had an appointment to meet with Dick Wolf's widow that afternoon.

All of a sudden, Eve gasped. "I almost forgot. I brought some cards from the gallery about my exhibit that Jack had printed. There's even a reproduction of one of my paintings on the front." She reached into her bag, grabbed two cards, then handed one to Peggy and another to Arthur.

"How lovely," replied Peggy. "Thank you. I'm really sorry I missed your reception, but, I'll be sure to go and see your paintings this week."

"Yes, thank you," echoed Arthur. "You're a good artist." His words were short and simple and Eve wondered if he'd even looked at her work. Like so many others who came to the gallery, she thought he seemed much more interested in Dick Wolf's murder.

As she was returning home, Eve took several deep breaths, then began thinking about what she'd just heard. *On the surface, paradise is beautiful*, she thought, *but, underneath, all is not what it appears to be*. Did Donna go with Valerie to Dick Wolf's office? And, if so, why didn't Valerie mention it? Is she hiding something, or did she simply think it wasn't important? Is Jack lying about Tommy's relationship to him? If so, why? She wondered if she should share any of what she'd just heard with Adam, then decided against it. *After all*, she thought, *everything people are saying is mere hearsay and conjecture*. Nothing is factual. He doesn't have any answers and he doesn't particularly enjoy hearing gossip.

Once inside her house, Eve showered, dressed, then made herself another cup of coffee and walked out to the patio. Coco followed closely behind her, waiting to see what would happen next. Just as she made herself comfortable in front of her easel, she heard Adam turn into the driveway.

"Another stimulating workout," he exclaimed, as he opened the patio gate and walked over to his wife.

"You should think about joining me some time. The gym has a nice mix of men and women and they have all sorts of equipment. You might like a change from the pool."

"No, thanks. I'll just wait until we get our exercycle and bikes. That will be quite enough exercise for me," replied Eve, as she continued sipping her coffee.

"You'll be happy to know that I took some of your cards with me and handed them out," continued Adam. "A couple of people said they'd like to go to the gallery and see what you've done. I'm trying to do my share to promote you," he added, with a smile.

"That's great. I appreciate it," Eve replied, casually. She was still deep in thought, rehashing what she'd heard at the pool and wondering how she was going to approach Valerie regarding Donna, or, if she should even ask any questions.

"I see they've been at it again," Adam remarked, snidely.

"Who's that? What are you talking about?" Eve asked, quizzically.

"The people at the pool. I know you too well, my dear. I can tell when you're deep in thought and I know the pool is the center of local gossip. That's why I thought you might enjoy the gym, as a change of pace. I didn't hear a word about Dick Wolf the whole time I was there and nobody asked me any annoying questions."

"It's nothing," said Eve, as she waved her hand. "Anyway, I'm glad you're home. It's almost time for me to go over to the restaurant to see Valerie. She's been doing a lot of redecorating and wants my opinion about a few things."

"Good," replied Adam. "While you're gone, I'm going to get back to my stamps. I met a man at the gym who's also a collector and we shared a good deal of stamp gossip. After that, I suppose I better finish our tax return."

"Will we owe anything?" asked Eve.

"Not for last year. But, who knows what this year will look like, once we see how many paintings you sell. Be sure to save all your art supply receipts. We will definitely need them."

"No problem. I always charge my supplies. That helps me keep track of everything," replied Eve.

Adam turned and entered the house, closely followed by Eve and Coco.

"Just one question," began Eve hesitantly, "do you think Tommy is really Jack's nephew?"

"Yes," replied Adam, curtly, without adding anything else, or asking any questions, then went into the bathroom to take a shower.

Eve smiled. "I could have predicted that," she whispered softly to Coco.

When he came out of the shower, Adam walked over to Eve and began to speak. "I've known you for so many years and every time I see that far away look on your face, it worries me and, lately, I've seen it quite a bit. I know you're not thinking about your art show and I know all the talk you hear at the pool can be upsetting. For your own sake, I wish you'd try to put all unpleasant thoughts out of your mind." His voice was gentle and caring, but firm.

"I just wish the sheriff would get on this case and wrap it up. That would help put a stop to all the idle gossip . . . at least for a while. I'd also love to see George Gomez get his name cleared. I worry about him."

"I'm sure the case will be solved at some point, but, there's nothing you or I can do. Right now, we need to try and forget about it and just let the sheriff do his job," replied Adam, then turned and left the room.

At quarter to one, Eve picked up her bag and walked into the den to let her husband know she was leaving. "I shouldn't be very long . . . have fun with your stamps."

"Don't forget what I told you," replied Adam, without looking up.

"I never forget what you tell me," said Eve, cheerfully.

Once she arrived at the restaurant, Eve was surprised to see that the Crazy Cactus sign had already been removed. Upon entering, she was greeted by Valerie.

"Thank you for coming on such short notice. I've so much to show you," said the woman, as she escorted Eve inside. "Donna and I have been very busy and we've made quite a few changes, as you will see. I hope you like them."

Eve looked around and noticed that the blue and white tile tables had been rearranged. She also observed that many of the paintings that previously hung on the walls had been removed, but, her stolen canvas remained in the same spot where she'd first caught sight of it. Overall, the large dining room maintained its Mexican flavor, but appeared simpler and less cluttered. She was pleased with what she observed.

"I can see that you've been very busy in here and I like what you've done," she remarked. "I notice you've taken down some of the paintings that hung on the wall. Do you think there are any other stolen ones, besides mine?"

"No, I'm pretty sure yours is the only one," Valerie replied, reassuringly. "The others were already hanging here, before Dick bought the restaurant, so he didn't have anything to do with them."

"That's good to know. I'd hate for people to start lining up, claiming they want their paintings back," remarked Eve.

"That reminds me . . . would you like to have your painting back . . . or, can I pay you for it?" asked Valerie.

"Oh, no, please keep it . . . that is, if you want it. The gallery's insurance covered my loss. I'm happy to leave it hanging here," Eve answered quickly, then continued speaking. "Are you also going to change the menu?"

"No," responded Valerie. "From everything I gather, people really enjoy the food here and I want to keep it that way. I'm re-hiring the same cook, as well as most of the staff. They're very familiar with both the restaurant and many of the regular customers. I know they'll help make the place a success."

"I think that's a good idea," said Eve. "I've heard so many positive reports from people. They really enjoy the food here, as well as the service."

"I have no doubt we'll attract many of the regulars, but, I'm afraid we'll also get our share of curiosity seekers," replied Valerie.

As Eve continued looking around, Donna and George Gomez emerged from the kitchen and walked towards her.

"I'm so glad you were able to come," said Donna. "As you can see, we're making some changes, and George has been such a big help."

"Oh, George, I was so happy to hear that you have your job back," Eve remarked, as she smiled broadly at the man.

"Yes, so am I," replied George. "Valerie and Donna have been very good to me. I can't tell you how relieved I am to be back at work again. It's been very difficult both for me and my family. Now, if I can just get my name cleared, everything will be perfect. You can't imagine all the people who come up to me and thank me for killing Mr. Wolf. Even though I tell them

I didn't do it, they still keep coming. And, I hate to say it, but even my children are getting heckled in school."

"Let's hope the sheriff can get things straightened out," added Donna. "Did Val tell you that we have a new name for the restaurant?" she asked, changing the subject.

"No, she didn't, but, I saw the sign was down when I drove up," replied Eve. "I'm curious. What have you decided to call this lovely place?"

"Sunshine Flower," answered Valerie, proudly. "The new sign is being made, as we speak. It should be ready in a couple of days. I wanted a name that's a little more upbeat. What do you think? How do you like it?"

"I can't wait to eat at the Sunshine Flower. Yes . . . I like it," replied Eve.

"Why don't you take Eve on a tour and show her some of the changes we've made so far," interjected Donna.

"My thought, exactly," replied Valerie. "Come on Eve . . . follow me. I'll give you the grand tour. I want to hear your valued opinion."

Eve followed behind Valerie, as they headed towards the rear of the restaurant and down the long hallway.

"First, as you can see, we took down some of the paintings that were hanging in the dining room and put them up here. Then, we added brighter lighting. So many people come down this hall and I think it was too dark. Now, it's much more cheerful. Take a look at what we've done in here," said Valerie, as she opened the door to the infamous office. "It's not at all the way you last saw it. Everything is new. I don't want to have any reminders of Dick. The sheriff's men ripped up the carpet, so I had this tile put in. The desk is new and in a different position. There's nothing remaining from the old office. I even replaced the file cabinets. What do you think?"

"It's very nice," replied Eve, "and you're right about the hallway. It's much more upbeat. I see you also removed all the rules and instructions from the door," she added, with a smile.

"Yes, I don't want people to be afraid to come in . . . just my name will suffice. When a door is closed, I find that people generally knock before entering. They don't need a sign to tell them what to do."

"I'm surprised there wasn't a camera in this office," remarked Eve.

"Dick was always so sure of his own power. I don't think he felt he needed one, but I'm thinking of installing one," replied Valerie.

"That might be a good idea, given what's happened. It certainly wouldn't hurt." Eve wanted to ask Valerie about Donna and thought this might be an appropriate time. "You know, I have a question that I've been meaning to ask you. I hope you don't mind."

"Go ahead . . . shoot, if you'll pardon my choice of words," replied Valerie, with a laugh.

"Well," began Eve, with some hesitation, "when you told me about your visit here to bring a box to your ex-husband, I got the impression that you were alone. Were you? Or did Donna come with you? It's probably none of my business, but I'm just curious."

"Actually, now that you ask, she did come with me," replied Valerie, sheepishly. "She never came into the office, however."

"I waited in the hallway," added Donna, who had joined them and stood in the doorway. "I wanted to make sure that man didn't try to hurt Val. I had no desire to go inside, or to see him. I just remained outside, waiting, quietly, to make certain there was no trouble."

"Yes . . . that's exactly what happened," said Valerie. "I didn't mention it to you or to the sheriff, because I didn't want Donna to be involved in all the chaos. She didn't see or hear anything. She was simply there to protect me, should Dick give me any grief. However, this time, there weren't any problems. He appeared to be busy with some paperwork, so, I just handed him the box and turned around. I don't think we exchanged more than two words. When I came out, Donna and I both left the restaurant together and, as I told you, Dick was very much alive."

"That makes sense," replied Eve. "Once again, please forgive me for asking."

"I'd appreciate it if you don't tell anyone about this, except your husband," added Valerie. "You know how quickly word travels around here and people tend to make up their own stories."

"Of course . . . I won't say a word to anyone," Eve assured her.

"Okay . . . onward," continued Valerie. "Let me show you the banquet room. That's where I intend to hang your paintings." She led Eve out and into the main dining room, then turned right and opened another door.

"This will be perfect," said Eve, as she entered the room.

"It's not a large room, but I think it will be ideal for small dinner parties. Your paintings will add a lot to the ambience. Jack Slater told me I should be able to pick them up in a couple of days. I'm anxious to get them up. They'll make such a difference in here."

"I can't get over how lovely everything looks," Eve remarked, with enthusiasm. "You've really been hard at work and I love all the changes you've made."

"Yes, we've all been very busy. Now, let's go back into the dining room. I have something I want to ask you. This is the main reason I was hoping you could come here today."

"I can't wait," replied Eve.

As they returned to the dining room, Valerie continued speaking. "You see that blank wall?" she asked, pointing to the back of the room. "It's directly in line with the entrance and is one of the first things people notice, when they come in. Well, I was wondering if I could commission you to do a large painting of a flower . . . to highlight the new name of the restaurant and to add some bright color to the room. I'd like to hang it on that wall."

"Oh, Valerie, this is so unexpected," gasped Eve. "You already bought three of my paintings . . . and now, you want another one? Are you sure?"

"Absolutely. I've given this a great deal of thought. I love what you do and I know a lot of folks appreciate your work, as well. I'll be willing to pay you two thousand dollars . . ."

"No . . . that's way too much." Eve didn't let her finish. "I'd love to do a painting for you, but I couldn't possibly accept your offer."

"But, I want to pay you. How much do you suggest?"

"How large a painting would you like?" asked Eve.

"Well, it just so happens that I bought a canvas. Let me show you." She turned and called out, "George, could you bring me that big blank canvas, near the window?"

A few seconds later, George Gomez emerged from the kitchen, carrying a large canvas. "Here it is," he said and placed it, carefully, against the wall in question.

"I was hoping you'd agree to my request, so I bought this for you to use," said Valerie, with a wide smile. "Now . . . I do want to pay you. How much are you willing to accept? Please tell me what you consider a fair offer . . . and, don't be modest."

Eve walked over to the wall and looked at the canvas. After reflecting for several seconds, she replied. "I think one thousand dollars would do it, but no more. How soon do you need it?"

"We'll probably be opening in a couple of weeks. It would be nice if we could have it up by then. Do you think it's possible? Or, would you like more time?"

"No problem." Eve's words were slow and precise. "I'm not working on anything else right now, so it shouldn't take me more than a couple of days. I usually paint pretty quickly and, since I'm not working on anything else at the moment, I can get started right away."

"Wonderful. I had a feeling you'd agree to my proposition. Now, since this is a larger canvas than what I saw at the gallery, do you think you have enough paint?"

"I hope so. If not, I always know where to get more."

"Spoken like a true artist," replied Valerie, with a smile. "George can bring the canvas out to your car."

"I'll call you when I'm finished," continued Eve. "As I said, it won't take me long. I'm going to love doing it. I even think I have something in mind that would be perfect in here . . . a nice large, colorful flower in my early Georgia O'Keeffe style. I think it will be just right for this room."

"Sounds good and I'll leave it up to you. I trust your judgment. Thanks so much, Eve. I really appreciate your help and I can't wait to see the finished work. As I said, we'll probably be opening in about two weeks. You and Adam must come . . . as my guests."

"Of course. I look forward to it," replied Eve.

After a few minutes, George picked up the canvas and followed Eve to her car. "You can just put it in here," she said, and opened the trunk.

As he was about to go back into the restaurant, George turned and spoke to Eve. "Thank you again for all your support. I really appreciate it, as does my wife. We've had a pretty rough time lately and I'm thankful for all the help I can get," he said, in a somber tone.

"You're so welcome. We have to keep thinking positively. I know the sheriff's working on the case and I'm sure it will be cleared up soon." Eve tried her best to sound encouraging, even though she had difficulty believing her own words.

On her way home, Eve began planning how she was going to complete her new assignment. Once she was back in her own house, she walked into the den to tell Adam the good news.

Looking up from his computer, he asked, "Well? No more problems, I hope."

"Au contraire, mon cher. For your information, I have just been commissioned to do a painting for the restaurant," replied Eve, then went on to summarize her meeting with Valerie.

"Terrific. I can see that this is just the beginning of a new career for you," said Adam, as he raised himself up from the desk. "I'll bring the canvas inside. I'm sure you're eager to get started."

"Even though I can see a finished product in my mind's eye, I'm not going to do any actual painting today . . . maybe just a sketch."

As Eve began to relax, she reviewed everything that had transpired during her visit to the restaurant. She thought Valerie had made some good changes and she was pleased that George had his job back. Although Eve was happy for George, she wished she could help clear his name. But, she didn't know where to begin.

There were at least thirty people who had both a motive and an opportunity to kill Dick Wolf, and she didn't know most of them. She also didn't like the fact that a killer was on the loose in Sunshine Valley and, since a gun was involved, he—or she—could kill again. Even though she'd tried her best to reassure George, she wondered if the sheriff was actively doing anything to resolve matters, or if this was just considered another cold case.

All of a sudden, the image of Donna popped into Eve's head. *She seemed rather quiet today*, she thought, *and didn't exhibit much enthusiasm. Stop it!* she chided herself. Donna was probably just tired from all the work she's been doing. Eve felt she was becoming more and more obsessed with the murder of Dick Wolf and she didn't like the way it made her feel. Finally, she began to breathe deeply, then managed to push all negative thoughts out of her mind and focus on the painting that was the big project for the morning.

Chapter 8

Eve Iverson's life had taken a very different direction over the past week from the one she'd planned for herself, when she and her husband moved to Sunshine Valley. After settling into their new home, she had every intention of relaxing and learning German, in preparation for a future trip to Europe. Although she enjoyed painting, she thought it would only be a part-time activity. Never, in her wildest imagination, did she think she would have a one-woman show of her paintings and now, a commission. She'd promised Valerie that it wouldn't take long to complete her assignment and this was a promise she intended to keep.

For the following two days, Eve resolved to focus on painting and not obsess about Dick Wolf and all the gossip that was floating around.

On Monday morning, she arose early and carried her blank canvas out to her patio studio. After applying gesso and while waiting for it to dry, she began to do some pencil sketches on her pad. She was soon joined by Adam, who was preparing to go to the gym.

"I can't wait to see what you turn out this time," he remarked, with a smile. "Whatever you do, I know it will be beautiful."

"Hopefully, you'll get to see it tomorrow," replied Eve, then continued. "Although Valerie didn't ask me to do it, I've been thinking that it would be nice to put a frame around this painting. Jack was so right about the benefit of frames. You're off to the gym, right?"

"Yes, I'm going a little early today, why? Is there something you need?"

"Do you think you could stop by the lumber yard on your way home and pick up some pieces of wood?" asked Eve. "Maybe you could make a simple frame for her painting."

"No problem. Let me measure the canvas," said Adam. "I'll get some thin strips and put them together. It won't be difficult. He turned and went into the work shed, then rolled out the tape measure. "That should do it," he said, as he sized the canvas. "I'll pick up the wood, after I'm finished running and bicycling. I can even paint the frame, if you like."

"I think a plain white one would be good. I don't want to detract from the painting itself, just enhance it."

"Okay. I'll see you in a little while," said Adam, as he turned and headed out.

Once the gesso dried, Eve began to fill in the canvas. She always said she preferred acrylic paints to oil, because they dried faster and she could continue painting without having to wait very long. For this project, she didn't want to do anything that was too realistic, or too abstract, and was pleased with what she saw developing. *This will be perfect for the restaurant*, she thought. As she continued applying bright colors to the large flower, she spotted a tiny lizard scampering across the patio. Ordinarily, Coco would run after it, but she just continued lying on the floor next to Eve, with her eyes tightly closed.

Eve was thankful that the stillness of the desert enabled her to concentrate on painting and put all other thoughts aside. Then, suddenly, she heard someone calling her name. She looked up and spotted Jackie, who was racing across the path from Frank's house, waving something in the air that resembled a pamphlet.

"Hi, Jackie," responded Eve. "You seem very excited. What's up?"

"I have something I'd like to show you."

"Come on in. The gate's unlocked."

Suddenly, Coco awakened and sprang to her feet, wagging her tail, as the woman entered the back patio gate and walked towards Eve.

"Look . . . look at this. It's a brochure that describes the Alaskan cruise Frank and I are going to take," exclaimed Jackie, with excitement. "Look at the pictures. It's going to be such a beautiful trip. I'm really looking forward to it and I can hardly wait."

"Be careful. Don't come too close. The canvas is still wet," Eve warned, as she got up. After scanning the booklet that Jackie handed her, Eve smiled broadly. "You're going to have a wonderful trip. I envy you."

"It won't be long now, only about another week, but I wish we were going tomorrow. I have to start packing. I hope I have enough clothes. They serve lovely dinners every night . . . and then, they have dances afterwards. Frank seems very casual about everything, but I'm thrilled."

"As long as you're here," said Eve, changing the subject, "how do you like my painting? It still needs a few finishing touches, but I think you'll get the idea."

"It's great. Is it for the gallery?"

Eve slowly began to explain. "No. I've been commissioned to do a painting for Dick Wolf's widow and the new restaurant. She's re-doing so much, including changing the name. My painting is going to hang in the Sunshine Flower. Once it re-opens, we'll have to go there for lunch or dinner."

All of a sudden, the smile on Jackie's face disappeared and she became very serious. "I don't think so," she replied, with hesitation. "You can go there, but

I'm a little leery of eating in a restaurant where a man was murdered . . . too many bad vibes."

"There won't be any trace of Dick Wolf in the new place. You wouldn't even recognize it. I think we're going to have to try and put the past out of our minds and enjoy the present," responded Eve, attempting to sound reassuring.

As suddenly as she appeared, Jackie turned and headed back towards the gate. "Thanks for listening to me," she said, over her shoulder, as she made a quick exit. "I have to get back. Frank is waiting for me."

Well, that was quick, thought Eve. *She's certainly focused on her trip. She barely looked at my painting.*

Just as she was applying the finishing touches to her colorful flower, Adam walked out on to the patio. "I'm back and I think I have everything we need for a suitable frame," he said, as he held several thin strips of wood in one hand and a can of paint in the other.

"Wonderful," replied Eve. "I've made great progress and, the way it looks, I'm sure I'll be finished tomorrow morning. We can put it on then. Will you be going to the gym again?"

"No, not tomorrow. I'm going to skip a day. I want to see if I can assemble your frame. The man at the lumber yard cut the right sizes, so it shouldn't take too long. I can paint the wood today, then taper the edges and nail it together, after you finish. You didn't promise to bring the painting tomorrow, did you?"

"No. I thought I'd bring it over on Wednesday. Even though I want Valerie to have the painting as soon as possible, I need to make sure everything is just right. After all, a lot of people are going to be seeing it."

"Once again . . . spoken like a true artist," replied Adam, as he turned, brought his purchases into the shed, then went into the house to take a shower.

After working for another hour, Eve decided it was time to quit. She closed her paint tubes, then sat back and looked carefully at what she'd accomplished. When she was satisfied, she picked up the canvas and carried it over to a wall, careful not to smudge any of the paint, before it dried.

When she entered the house, Adam greeted her with a smile. "You had a phone call from Jack," he said, with enthusiasm. "If you come by Wednesday morning, he'll have a nice check for you. So far, eight paintings have sold . . . that's four thousand dollars . . . just for you."

"Wow! And then, I'll get another check for one thousand dollars from Valerie for my commission," replied Eve, with a broad smile. "I can't believe how the money keeps rolling in."

"You certainly have had a productive few days. I must admit, it feels good to be married to a wealthy woman," teased Adam.

"Wait and see. Although it's taking some time for all of my new found success to sink in, I think this is just the beginning of a very different and prosperous career for me."

"I want to paint the wood for the frame now, so everything will be ready to go when you think you're finished," said Adam, as he walked out to the patio.

After they completed their projects for the day, Adam and Eve spent a quiet, uninterrupted evening. They retired earlier than usual and had a restful night's sleep.

The following morning, Eve awakened early and was up before Adam. "Are you going to sleep all morning?" she chided her husband, as he began to stir.

"No. . . I want to put together the frame for your canvas and then, I even planned on doing some more gardening. Aren't you proud of me?" he said, with a yawn.

"Good. Come outside when you're ready. I just have a few minor touch-ups to make."

After downing a quick breakfast, Eve went out to the patio and looked at her painting. *Maybe I should leave well enough alone,* she thought, then went back inside.

It didn't take long for Adam to join her. "Are you ready?" he asked.

"Ready and waiting. I'm eager to see how the painting will look with the frame around it," replied Eve.

Adam assembled the pieces of wood and nailed them to the canvas in under an hour. "I think this should do it," he said, then leaned it against the wall, waiting for Eve's approval.

"Fabulous," replied Eve. "I can't get over the difference a frame makes. It really does enhance the painting. I think Valerie is going to be very pleased when she sees this."

"I'm sure she'll love it, as will the hundreds of others who will be coming to the restaurant. I'm very proud of you," said Adam, as he put his arm around his wife's shoulder.

"Will you be going to the gym again tomorrow?" asked Eve. "If so, we need to coordinate our schedules."

"No. I decided to skip another day. I know you want to bring your painting over to the restaurant, so, you can take the car. As long as I've started, I'd like to finish the gardening. I'll get back to my regular exercise schedule on Thursday."

"Great. I shouldn't be too long. My first stop will be the gallery, to pick up the check. Then, I'll head over to the restaurant to deliver the painting . . . and to pick up another check," she said, cheerfully.

Once again, the Iversons spent a peaceful afternoon and evening, with no interruptions.

On Wednesday morning, as promised, Eve prepared to deliver her painting to Valerie at the Sunshine Flower restaurant, while Adam went out to the patio to do some weeding.

After placing the canvas in the trunk of her car, Eve headed for the shopping center. She was pleased to have been so involved with painting for the past two days. By doing so, she didn't have an opportunity to dwell on the unpleasant events that had recently occurred. But, as she was driving, she recalled how she and Adam had driven to the Crazy Cactus, anticipating a simple lunch, then spotting her stolen painting, then finding the body of Dick Wolf. She thought it ironic that the discovery of her stolen painting had led to such negative, as well as positive, outcomes. If all had gone as originally planned, she might not have had an art exhibit, she wouldn't have met Valerie, and she wouldn't have been commissioned to do another painting. Now, her large painting, as well as three smaller ones, were going to receive a permanent home in the very place that was the scene of such turmoil.

As she continued driving, Eve had the eerie sensation that something wasn't quite right, but she was unable to identify exactly what it was. *Perhaps Jackie has a point,* she thought, *perhaps, even though Valerie has made many changes, the restaurant might still have some bad vibes.* Finally, as she neared the parking lot, she was able to push these negative thoughts out of her mind.

All of sudden, Eve realized that the art gallery was supposed to be her first stop. She had been so mentally distracted, she almost forgot. She made a quick U-turn, then headed for the Sunshine Gallery at the opposite end of the shopping center.

As she stepped out of the car and walked up to the gallery, Jack opened the door and led her inside. "Good," he said. "I'm glad you're here. I have to leave soon, but I wanted to make sure you got your check," he added, with a broad smile.

"Uncle Jack, did you see where I put my black bag?" asked Tommy, as he emerged from the back room. "Oh . . . Eve . . . I didn't hear you come in. So nice to see the successful artist again. You really had a good show. We'll have to do it again."

"Yes, she certainly did. Wait here. I have something for you," said Jack, as he went back to his office, then emerged a few seconds later, waving a check in the air. "Here you are, madam . . . four thousand dollars. I'll probably have more for you again soon. People really love your work."

Eve graciously accepted the check and put it in her purse. She looked over at Tommy, who was, once again, dressed in his cowboy regalia. However, this time, she noticed he was wearing a gun in his holster. "What's with the gun?" she asked, cautiously. "Is it real or is it a toy?"

"Not a toy," laughed Tommy. "I'm too old for toys, but it's all legit. Even though it's not required in this state, I made sure I registered it. I don't want any problems, in case it gets stolen. I'm going to the shooting range this morning. I enjoy doing a little target practice whenever I have some free time."

"I see," replied Eve. "Your last name isn't, by any chance, Gunn, is it?"

Tommy laughed. "I get asked that question sometimes, mostly by Uncle Jack's friends. He's the only one who calls me Tommy. My real name is Tom Henderson."

"Yes, this is my Tommy," interjected Jack. "I just wish my sister, his mother, were alive today, to see her beautiful grown son. He really turned out to be a winner. I'm so proud of him and pleased that he's here to help me in the gallery."

"Well, I'm off to see if I can score some points now. I know I'll see you again soon, so, bye for now," said Tommy, as he looked at Eve, then turned and exited.

Eve was also eager to make a quick departure. "I'm sure we both have other things to do," she declared, "so I'll be on my way. Give me a call if, and when, you want me to pick up the rest of my paintings."

"Actually, I was thinking that, although your exhibit officially ends in another week, we could keep them hanging up through the summer. It's usually kind of quiet around here and I don't have anything planned, but, just in case a potential buyer happens to wander in, I'd like to be able to show your paintings."

"That's fine with me. It's better that they're here, rather than in my storeroom," replied Eve, with a laugh. "And, thank you so much for the check. This will come in very handy."

As she left the gallery and drove over to the restaurant, Eve smiled. *Well, that settles that question,* she thought. Tommy is definitely Jack's nephew. At least one mystery has been solved.

Once again, as she got into her car and began driving towards the restaurant, she had a queasy feeling, but was unable to explain the reason for it. She tried her best to keep her mind focused on the positive events that were occurring.

"Hello," Eve called out, as she entered the Sunshine Flower. She spotted Valerie, who was leaving her office and walking down the hallway.

"I thought you might be coming this morning. How did it go? Did you do another masterpiece?" asked the woman.

"Yes, indeed. I have the finished objet d'art in my car. Is George here? Or, can you help me carry it in?"

"George is out doing a couple of errands. He should be back shortly, but I can help you. I'm anxious to see what you've done," replied Valerie.

The two women went out to Eve's car and carried the painting into the restaurant.

"This is fabulous. It's just what this room needs. Let's hang it over here," said Valerie, as they walked towards the rear wall. "George already put up the brackets."

The two women hung the canvas and stepped back to see if any adjustments were needed. "It's perfect. I love the bright colors . . . and, look, you framed me, as well," Valerie added with a laugh.

Although Eve didn't appreciate the woman's choice of words, she said nothing. She simply scanned her painting and was pleased with what she saw.

"I can't wait 'til Donna and George see your work... and all the customers," continued Valerie. "It's a perfect finish to the room."

"Where is Donna?" asked Eve. "Is she okay?"

"Oh, yes, she's fine," replied Valerie. "She's in Tucson today, getting her things together and then she'll be back . . . to stay. I'm so happy with the way things are going. Jack Slater called me and said I could pick up your other three paintings from the gallery tomorrow. Do you think it's possible for you to stop by here . . . perhaps in the afternoon? I'm going to hang them in the banquet room and I'd love to get your opinion. I hope it's not asking too much."

"No, of course not. I'd love to see what you have planned. I'll give you a call first," replied Eve.

"Now, before you leave," continued Valerie, "I have something for you." She went into the kitchen and quickly returned, waving a check in her hand. "This is for you . . . with great appreciation."

"Thank you so much. I really enjoyed doing the work and I look forward to seeing it many times," said Eve, as she placed the check in her purse.

Just as she was getting ready to leave, George Gomez came rushing through the front door. He was sweating and gasping for air.

"What is it, George?" asked Valerie, in an alarmed voice. "What happened? Are you okay?" She rushed over to the man, who appeared to be on the verge of collapse. "Let me help you. Sit down here . . . in this chair."

Eve joined the two of them, shaken by George's sudden entry. "Take a deep breath and just try to relax... then, tell us what's wrong," she said, in her most comforting voice.

After a few minutes, George slowly began to speak in a deep, somber tone. "I think somebody just tried to kill me. When I parked the car and got out, another car came speeding towards me and almost ran over me. There were two men inside. One of them shouted out the window, 'Killer. We know you're a killer. You deserve to die too.' I fell down, but barely escaped being run over." He was gasping for air, as he related what had just occurred.

"You stay here, George, and try to calm down. You're safe now. I'll bring you something to drink," said Valerie, then turned and ran into the kitchen. She returned a minute later with a glass and a pitcher full of water.

George filled the glass and finished it immediately. "I was so scared," he said, slowly. "I thought, for sure, I'd be run down by those men. I'm lucky to be alive."

"Should we call the sheriff?" asked Valerie. "We could all be targets. These men are dangerous and should be reported. We need to let him know what happened."

"No, please don't call him," protested George. "I don't want to face the sheriff and his men again. Anyway, I wouldn't be able to help them very much. I didn't get a license plate number and I couldn't describe the men, or the car. Everything happened so fast. They're gone now, thank goodness. I just hope they don't come back and try to kill me." He continued drinking water and slowly began to compose himself, then continued. "I don't want my wife to know about this, either. It would be too upsetting for her. She's already heard enough of my problems. Some people have been cheering me on, now others are trying to kill me. I wish the sheriff would find the real killer and end this mess. I can't tell you what it's done to me and my family. I want it all to be over."

Eve thought there was very little she could say to console the man and remained quiet, but she began thinking. She felt she'd waited long enough and that it was time to do some serious sleuthing. Not only did George need to be cleared of murder, but, she thought the restaurant and everyone in it could also be in danger. She even felt that she was indirectly responsible for George's troubles. If she, Adam, and Maria, hadn't seen him run out of Dick Wolf's office, he wouldn't be considered a 'person of interest' and people wouldn't be harassing him, or trying to hurt him. She believed it was time for her to act.

"You're safe now, but, you need to sit here for a while, until you feel stronger," said Valerie, softly.

"I know he had quite a few enemies, but did your husband happen to have any *friends* that you know of?" Eve asked Valerie.

"He did have a couple of misfits that he ran around with, but I never met them and I'm afraid I don't even know their names. Do you think they could be the ones who came after George?"

"I have no idea. It was just a thought," replied Eve. "Now, I think I'm going to leave you two. Val is right, George. Just try to relax until you feel better." After a short pause, she looked at Valerie and spoke. "I'll see you tomorrow afternoon, but I'll give you a call first."

Eve made her exit and looked around to make sure there weren't any suspicious looking vehicles waiting in the parking lot. Once she felt it was safe, she walked to her car and started for home.

As she was driving, Eve took several deep breaths, then began reviewing the events that had just taken place. She wondered if she should share them with Adam. *Of course*, she thought. This isn't gossip or rumor. It's reality. She felt an increasing need to do something helpful, something that would put an end to the chaos that appeared to be increasing, but she was at a loss as to where to begin.

Once she arrived at her house, Eve was immediately greeted by Adam. "Well, how did it go?" he asked, cheerfully.

"Good . . . and bad," she replied, in a serious tone.

"Not again. You seem upset. Tell me what happened."

"First, the good," said Eve as she took out her two checks and waved them. "Here's five thousand dollars. Eight paintings were sold and one commission. I can hardly believe my art work has generated so much money in such a short time. Val loved my flower and it fits in perfectly in the restaurant."

"That's wonderful. Now, I'm almost afraid to ask..."

Eve didn't let him finish and began to recount the incident with George Gomez at the restaurant.

"Didn't anyone call the sheriff?" Adam asked, in disbelief.

"George didn't want to deal with him again," replied Eve. "I can't say I blame him."

After a brief discussion about the attack, Eve paused for a moment, then went on to talk about her meeting at the art gallery. "You were right. Tommy is Jack's nephew. Of that, I'm sure. I saw both of them at the gallery. Tommy was on his way to the shooting range. He seems like a nice enough fellow, but I'm a little concerned about his interest in guns. He was wearing one in his holster today. Although he said it was registered, it never occurred to me to ask about the caliber."

"A lot of people enjoy target practice. It doesn't mean they have any bad intentions, or that they use their weapons recklessly," replied Adam.

"I know, but, because of what has happened, I'm a bit more leery these days," sighed Eve.

"I didn't want to tell you this before," continued Adam, "but, perhaps I should do so now. When we were at your reception, you noticed that I was cornered by a few men. Most of them asked me questions about the discovery of Dick Wolf's body. But, one man said he was just arriving at the restaurant to have lunch with his wife that day, when he spotted two men wearing cowboy outfits walk in and head towards the back. He said he didn't pay much attention to them at the time, but, in the gallery, he recognized Jack Slater and his nephew, Tommy, as the same two men."

"Why didn't you want to tell me this before?" asked Eve, in disbelief.

"You were having such a nice reception and I thought it would be an unnecessary distraction," replied Adam. "But, now, I think you need to be careful when you're around either of these men. You probably shouldn't ask too many personal questions. If they had anything to do with Dick Wolf's murder, I don't want either of them to think you might suspect them."

"This is becoming more and more of a real nightmare and I fear things are getting worse . . ."

Adam didn't let her finish. "I know this is very upsetting, but, once again, you must try to focus on more pleasant things. That may sound too simple, but we have to let the sheriff do his job and hope for the best. There's not much we can do . . . just be careful and, if possible, try not to get more involved."

Eve listened and nodded, without saying a word. She disagreed with Adam's assessment and felt she had to do something, but knew there was no use arguing with her husband.

"I know you said you were going to the gym tomorrow morning . . . do you think you'll be back around noon?" asked Eve, slowly changing the subject.

"Yes . . . do you need the car again?"

"In the afternoon. Valerie is picking up my three paintings from the art gallery and asked me to stop by the restaurant. She wants to show me where she plans to hang them," replied Eve.

"I hope this isn't going to become a daily occurrence," Adam remarked, in a slight tone of impatience.

"No, not at all," said Eve. "She just wants my opinion about a few things before she re-opens. I don't feel I can refuse her requests, since she's been so generous with me. This will be a short visit and I won't be gone long."

"Now, how about sitting on the patio for a while and sipping a nice, cold glass of wine?" suggested Adam. "I think it would do you good."

"Brilliant idea." Finally, for the first time since she returned home, Eve managed to smile at her husband.

Chapter 9

The following morning, after Adam left for the gym, Eve was thankful that she could spend a leisurely few hours alone and not have to rush out early. She allowed herself to enjoy a large breakfast of scrambled eggs, bacon, and toast, something she hadn't done in a long time. After she finished eating, she went out onto the patio and played with Coco, something else she hadn't done for quite a while.

Despite the attempt to involve herself in normal activities, Eve couldn't escape thinking about all the events that had occurred since she and Adam discovered Dick Wolf's body. Numerous different faces flashed through her mind. *So many suspects*, she thought, *who had both motive and opportunity to kill the man*. Without a clue as to where to begin to solve this puzzle, she became increasingly suspicious of everyone, both people she knew, as well as those she didn't know.

Although she wasn't particularly eager to go to the restaurant again so soon, Eve had promised Valerie and felt she owed her at least one more visit. *A stop at the bank to deposit her checks would renew her enthusiasm*, she thought. After assessing her paint tubes, she decided she'd also go to the art supply store to replenish certain colors. This would give her the opportunity to purchase a gift certificate for Doty to help her get started painting.

"I'm home," called Adam, just as Eve was hanging up the phone.

"You're a little later today," she said to her husband, as he entered the den.

"I wasn't paying attention to the time," replied Adam. "I met someone new . . . a tourist from Omaha. He was on the treadmill next to me and we started talking. I know you're eager to be on your way, so I'll fill you in on our conversation when you return."

"I'll try to get this visit over with as quickly as possible, so you can tell me all about your workout," Eve said, with a smile, then left the house and began her short journey.

Once she arrived at the bank, Eve went inside and deposited her checks. *I think I'll have to make a copy of this and frame it*, she thought, as she proudly held up the receipt, then placed it carefully in her purse. After leaving the bank, she slowly drove to the art supply store, where she picked up a large jar of gesso and some tubes of red, blue, and yellow acrylic paints. Looking around to see if there was anything else she needed, she decided against purchasing any additional canvases. She thought she had enough blank ones at home and could always paint over one, if necessary. When she felt satisfied that she had everything she'd come for, she walked over to the cashier and purchased a gift certificate in the amount of two hundred dollars. *This should help Doty get started*, she thought.

After placing her supplies in the car, Eve drove off to meet with Valerie. Once again, she began to feel the same sense of anxiety she experienced before her last visit and hoped there wouldn't be any problems this time. Upon arriving at the restaurant, she noticed that the new sign was now up and hanging in place. Large and boldly colored, the *Sunshine Flower* stood out for everyone to see. As she slowly eased her way out of the car, she looked around to make certain no suspicious vehicles were lurking nearby. She was relieved to see that everything appeared normal and quiet.

Upon opening the restaurant door, Eve was immediately greeted, not only by Valerie, but Donna and George were also present and welcomed her. She quickly ran over to George and tried to control her apprehension, as she began to speak.

"How are you doing today, George?" Eve asked in a strained voice. "You look good. You had quite a shock, but I hope you're feeling better and have been able to recuperate a bit."

"I'm fine. No problems today . . . at least, not yet, but I'm being very careful," he replied, with a smile.

"That's wonderful. And you, Donna? I missed you yesterday, but I heard you were in Tucson. How is everything coming along? Are you getting settled in?"

"I finally have everything I need here," said Donna. "It's not easy hauling around all the junk we collect over the years. I'm sure you had the same experience when you moved to Sunshine Valley. This time, I've managed to throw out a lot of things I don't use any longer."

"Thank you, again, for coming," interjected Valerie. "Your three other paintings are now hanging up and ready to be viewed by the world. You'll have to tell me what you think."

"I really like this large one that you did," remarked Donna, as she pointed to the back wall. "I love the colors and I know people will also enjoy seeing it when they walk in. You're very talented."

"Thank you, but, I'm afraid all these compliments are going to my head," said Eve, with a laugh.

"You need to come back here," urged Valerie, as she took Eve by the hand and led her towards the rear of the restaurant. "I want to show you how the banquet room looks now."

Upon opening the door, Eve spotted her three paintings that were arranged on one brown wall. A long blue tile table took up most of the space in the relatively narrow room.

"It's a bit dull in here and I think your canvases will help make a more pleasant environment," remarked Valerie. "I may eventually get around to painting the walls white, but, for now, I'll leave them the way they are. There are just too many other more important things to do before we open."

After a pause, she invited Eve to take a seat, then pulled out a chair for herself on the opposite side of the table.

"I can picture many happy events taking place in this room," continued Valerie. "Dick hardly ever used it. Now, after making all these changes in the restaurant, I wonder what he would think."

"His opinion doesn't matter," replied Eve. "You've done a wonderful job and I'm so glad that you've included me."

Valerie had a very serious look on her face, as she continued speaking. For a second, Eve wondered if a confession was forthcoming, then chided herself for being so suspicious of everyone.

"Well," said Valerie, "his ashes are now scattered somewhere in the desert. I had one of our staff do it. I couldn't bear to do it myself and I didn't want to ask George. Although I wanted to pay him, the man said he didn't want to take any money. He said it would give him great pleasure to do me this favor. It's hard for me to believe that Dick is no longer here. I've been thinking about him a lot lately and, despite his nastiness, I've started to feel a little sorry for him. I can only imagine that he must have been a deeply unhappy man to behave the way he did. I wonder if he'd have been happier if he'd never left Milwaukee. At least, he would still be alive, but, then, if he'd stayed there, we wouldn't be sitting here now."

Eve hesitated for a moment, surprised at what she'd just heard. "Milwaukee? I thought you said he was from Houston."

"No. We met in Houston, when we were both working in the same restaurant, but he was from Milwaukee, originally . . . born and raised there," replied Valerie. "It's a nice city. I went there once with Dick, after we were married, just as he was beginning to turn on me. We stayed with his mother. He was gone most days, doing who knows what, so I had a good opportunity to get to talk with her. I liked her. She was very sweet . . . the total opposite of Dick. You would never suspect that he was her son. I told her about the change in her son's behavior that I'd begun to notice. She wasn't surprised. She said he was just like his father. He'd taught Dick to be tough, from early childhood. He'd said it was the only way he'd ever gain people's respect. When Dick was in school, he used to harass other children and would get into numerous fights . . . even with girls. One girl in particular got the brunt of his meanness. According to what his mother learned from teachers, Dick would continually run after the girl and claim she had a boy's name. He even tried to pull her clothes off, to prove she wasn't really a girl. He was a real bully."

Eve hesitated for a moment, then asked meekly, "By any chance, do you happen to remember the girl's name?"

"Johnnie . . . or Jamie . . . no, it was Jackie. I remember thinking that Jackie Kennedy probably never had such a problem with her name. That's it . . . Jackie. His mother said that she was often called to the principal's office, because of her son's actions. Apparently, he harassed the poor girl to such an extent, that she even stopped coming to school. I don't think Dick's behavior improved much over the years. In fact, in some ways, it may have gotten worse. As you've seen, so many folks around here are very glad he's dead . . . so much for respect. You know, Donna's mother was married to Dick for a short time and she died young. We've often wondered if he wasn't directly, or, at least, indirectly responsible for her death."

Eve was stunned by what she was hearing and was at a loss for words. She couldn't wait to return home and tell Adam what she'd just learned. She searched frantically for an excuse to leave. "I'm afraid I must be going. My husband needs to use the car," she finally said, as she slowly pushed herself up from the table.

"I hope I didn't upset you with all this talk about Dick," began Valerie.

"No, not at all. It's a sad story. I know he was a mean person, but, you didn't upset me," replied Eve, then quickly changed the subject. "But, before I go, I have to tell you, I'm very pleased with the way you're displaying my paintings. I hope they bring pleasure to the folks who'll be dining here." She felt her words sounded rather empty, but she was eager to leave.

As Eve made her exit and began to drive home, she kept reviewing in her mind everything Valerie had told her about her husband's early years. Could Jackie Quinn possibly be the girl he bullied as a child? Could she have been building up resentment all these years and finally sought revenge? Eve was deeply perplexed. She thought Jackie seemed so positive and happy. She certainly didn't seem like a killer. She wondered if Doty and Paula knew anything about Jackie's possible childhood encounters with Dick Wolf.

After pulling into her driveway, Eve slammed on the brakes and rushed into the house. Adam heard the noise and came quickly to hear if something had happened at the restaurant. "I'm almost afraid to ask," he said. "Is everything okay? How is George Gomez doing today?"

"George is fine, but, there's something else I need to tell you," replied Eve breathlessly. She braced herself, as Adam placed an arm around her waist in support. "I think I know who killed Dick Wolf," she said, as she gasped for air.

"Jackie Quinn," replied Adam, without hesitation.

"What? How and when did you find out? You must tell me." Eve was stunned. She couldn't believe her ears.

"Come here and sit down," said Adam, as he led his wife to the couch in the living room. "Before you went out, I mentioned that there was something I wanted to tell you. Well, when I was at the gym, I met a man I hadn't seen there before. He was on the treadmill next to me and we began talking. It seems that he was at the restaurant with his family the day Dick Wolf was killed. He told me that, after spilling some salsa on his shirt, he went to the men's room to clean it off. Naturally, I asked him if he saw or heard anything unusual. He said that, as he started down the hallway, he saw a woman in a red dress, leaving Dick's office. He noticed her, because he thought his wife would like what she was wearing and wanted to point out the woman after he came back to the table. But, when he returned and looked around, he didn't see her. He said she was attractive and had short curly black hair. She even smiled at him as they passed each other in the hallway. His description of the woman fits Jackie to a *t*."

"Unbelievable," remarked Eve. "Did he say if he heard a gun shot?"

"I asked him and he said there was a lot of noise coming from the dining room, but he never heard anything that sounded like a gun shot."

After a short pause, Eve began to recount everything Valerie had told her about Dick Wolf's childhood and how he'd continually harassed a girl named Jackie in grammar school.

"When we were at Frank's place for the barbecue, she said she went to the restaurant, just to pick up the flan," commented Adam, "but, she could easily have walked back to the office, without anyone noticing."

"And then shoot Dick Wolf? I wonder if she has a gun and, if so, where she got it," mused Eve.

"It's not very difficult for anyone to get a weapon these days," replied Adam.

"We have to do something," said Eve, firmly. "We need to talk with Jackie and see what she has to say. Perhaps she has a plausible explanation for anything that might have occurred. We have to tell her what we both heard. I find it so difficult to picture her as a killer. Perhaps it wasn't her, but if she did do it, she needs to turn herself in to the authorities. Oh . . . Adam, this is becoming more and more of a nightmare."

"Yes, we do need to talk with her . . . the sooner, the better. It's a bit late now, but I think we should go over to her place tomorrow," suggested Adam. "If she really is the person who killed Dick Wolf, I feel sorry for Frank. I think he'll be shocked. I can't imagine how he might react to the news."

"Let's not jump to any conclusions until we've spoken with Jackie," cautioned Eve.

"Well, you've provided the motive and I discovered the opportunity . . . I'm sorry to have to say it, but, based on what we've each learned, it's not looking good for Jackie."

"Let's wait and see. If she did shoot Dick Wolf, maybe she has a good explanation," replied Eve, in a hollow voice, but, she had difficulty believing her own words.

In the midst of their commiseration, the front door
bell rang.

"I'll get it," said Eve, as she pushed herself up.

Once again, when she opened the door, a smiling
Doty appeared, holding out a box. "Paula and I want
you to have these cookies. We baked them especially
for you. I know it's not much, but we want to thank you
for the painting that you gave us. We just love it."

Eve accepted the box and asked Doty to come
inside, as Coco began running around her in circles.
"Sit down for a while," she said, as she led her neighbor
into the living room.

"Look what Doty brought us . . . some cookies,"
announced Eve, to her husband.

"Chocolate chip," replied Doty, then seated herself
in an armchair.

"Yum," replied Adam. "I could go for a cookie right
now."

Eve opened the box, helped herself, then passed it on
to Adam. "Delicious," she said, as she began chewing.

"Good. Keep eating. We always have more," replied
Doty, with a smile.

"No, Coco," said Adam, as he patted the dog's head.
"This is not for you."

"I'm glad you stopped by," said Eve. "There's
something I've been meaning to ask you. By any
chance, did you know that Dick Wolf was from
Milwaukee . . . you know, the man who was killed at
the restaurant? Someone told me he was born and
raised there. Since you and Paula are also from
Milwaukee, I thought you might have heard this." She
continued chewing a cookie and tried to sound as casual
as possible. She had no intention of mentioning
anything about Jackie, not at this point.

"No. I never heard anything about him being from
Milwaukee," replied Doty. "That's a surprise. I read the

death notice in the paper. It didn't provide much information. It just gave his name and age and said that he was the owner of the Crazy Cactus restaurant. No funeral arrangements were planned. The notice was very short and it certainly didn't say anything about him being from Milwaukee. I watch the news regularly on television and I never heard anything about where he was from, originally. I'm sure Paula and Jackie don't know any more than I do. They would certainly have mentioned it."

"I was just curious," remarked Eve, flatly. "It seems like a lot of folks from Milwaukee enjoy coming to the desert."

"Yes, it's such a treat," remarked Doty. "I never regret a day that I've been here and certainly wouldn't want to return to all that cold weather, rain, and snow. Paula and I just love our home and I know Jackie is going to love it here too. She already does."

Suddenly, Eve's voice took on a happier tone, as she looked at Doty and spoke. "Now, I also have something for you." She'd been so preoccupied with the news about Jackie that she almost forgot to give her neighbor the gift certificate that she'd purchased for her.

"Just a minute. I'll be right back." She got up and went into the bedroom. When she returned, Eve handed the certificate to Doty. "This is for the budding artist. I saw your drawings and I heard some of your comments about composition and shapes, as you walked around the art gallery. I have a strong suspicion that there's a lot of artistic talent inside you that's just waiting to come out. You can use this to get started, perhaps buy some paints and a few canvases. I can't wait to see what you create."

"Oh, Eve," gasped Doty, as she looked at the document. "This is too much. You've already been so kind."

"Nonsense. We artists have to stick together and I believe it's your turn to show off," replied Eve, as she smiled broadly at her neighbor.

"Now, I don't have any excuses not to paint. This is very exciting. I can't wait to tell Paula. Maybe I'll even be able to give you a painting one day."

"Don't worry. For now, cookies are just fine," remarked Adam.

"Remember, we have more. Just let me know when you run out," replied Doty, amiably.

After another few minutes discussing what she might paint, Doty raised herself up and out of the chair. "I have to go now. I want to show this to Paula. She'll be so surprised."

Eve walked her friend to the door, then came back to the living room to face Adam.

"That was really nice of you," said Adam.

"I hope she has fun. But, back to Jackie." Eve's voice took on a much more serious tone. "I'm going to call her and see if she's available tomorrow morning. We have to talk with her. I hope this news won't upset her, but I'm really anxious to hear what she has to say."

"Yes, go ahead," replied Adam.

Eve left the room to make her phone call and returned a few minutes later.

"Well? What did she say? Is she available?" asked Adam.

"As usual, she was very cheerful and said she'd planned on going swimming in the morning, but she should be available around eleven. I said we'd stop by before noon. I'm afraid this is going to be a very difficult meeting. I'm not looking forward to it."

"Nor am I, but, it's something we must do. We have to be forthright, but very tactful," replied Adam. "I think we need to make a plan."

And so, the Iversons spent the remainder of the day and evening discussing how they were going to approach Jackie.

Chapter 10

On Saturday morning, the Iversons slowly prepared for their imminent encounter with Jackie Quinn. Although she lived within walking distance, they decided to take the car and drive over to her house. They feared they might run into one or more of their neighbors and were reluctant to stop and chat

Despite what she'd heard from Valerie and Adam, Eve still had difficulty believing her neighbor was a murderer. "I hope this isn't a mistake," she said, as they drove off. "Maybe we're wrong. Maybe she didn't do it."

"I'm surprised at you," replied Adam. "I thought you were anxious to help find the person who killed Dick Wolf and get George Gomez off the hook."

"Of course, I want to help George, but I'd hoped the killer was somebody we weren't so close to . . . somebody we didn't know personally," replied Eve, flatly. "Jackie seems so happy to be reunited with her lifelong friends Doty and Paula, to be living in Sunshine Valley, to have met Frank and, now, to be going on a cruise. It's just hard to imagine her as a killer."

"Remember what we discussed last night," warned Adam. "Don't say too much. If she *is* the one who pulled the trigger, we don't want to be accused of aiding and abetting. We need to simply encourage her to turn herself in to the authorities."

Upon arriving at their destination, Adam and Eve were greeted by a smiling Jackie, who immediately ushered them inside. "It's so nice of you both to stop by. I've been meaning to call you and have you come over."

"You're probably wondering why we want to see you," said Adam, somberly.

"I suppose you want to see where I've hung Eve's painting," replied Jackie, still smiling. "I just picked it up yesterday and Frank helped me hang it," she added.

Suddenly, Eve's heart started pounding, as she looked across the living room and spotted her canvas. It was hanging in a prominent place on the living room wall for everyone to see. At that moment, she wished she could turn around and leave.

"I love it," said Jackie, "and, I hope to get another one in the near future."

"Perhaps we better sit down," suggested Adam.

"You sound so serious," replied Jackie. "Is something the matter? Are Doty and Paula and Frank okay?"

"They're fine," replied Adam. "This is about you. We need to talk."

Adam and Eve each sat down in an armchair, while Jackie poised herself comfortably on the couch.

Although she felt a great deal of anxiety, Eve was the first to speak. "There's something we want to ask you, and I certainly hope you won't be offended. As you know, this is a small town and people tend to talk a lot. Sometimes, what they have to say is factual and sometimes, it's just sheer conjecture and gossip. So, again, please don't be offended by what we have to ask you—"

Jackie didn't let her finish. "Now, I'm really curious. What is it you want to ask me? Please . . . go ahead and ask anything you want."

"Well," continued Eve, as she carefully chose her words. "I know you were at the restaurant the day Dick

Wolf was killed and you said that you just went there to pick up the flan. But, someone saw you, or someone resembling you, come out of his office. Also, it appears that Mr. Wolf was originally from Milwaukee and used to harass other children when he was little, especially, a girl named . . . Jackie."

"You got me," replied Jackie, as she slapped her knees. "I was wondering how long it would take." Without a pause, she continued, "Yes, I'm the person who killed Dick Wolf. I thought you two would be the ones who'd figure it out. Paula told me how you solved the murder of Frank's wife Olive. I knew it was just a matter of time, before you discovered what I did."

Both Adam and Eve were astounded by what they were hearing. They looked at each other in silence, not knowing what to say next. Neither of them had anticipated such a quick and bold admission. They both wondered if Jackie was serious, or if she was joking.

Eve finally gained the courage to speak. "Do you want to tell us about it?"

"I'd be glad to. It's a long story and goes way back," replied Jackie.

"Why don't you start from the beginning," Eve said, encouragingly.

"Well, I knew Dick Wolf in grammar school . . . not the one where I met Doty and Paula, but, the first one I attended. We were in the same grade and he used to taunt me every day. He said I had a boy's name and that I wasn't really a girl, so why was I wearing dresses? He chased me and hit me and continually tried to pull off my clothes. He'd even follow me into the girl's bathroom and harass me. It got so bad that I stopped going to school. I became more and more withdrawn and, at one point, I even thought about killing myself. Then, one day, my parents moved and they enrolled me in a new school. It was the happiest day of my life.

Even though things got much better, I was still afraid Dick Wolf would come after me and, sure enough, he did, but when I was older. I'd run into him, from time to time, and he continued to threaten me. He was a real monster. When I moved to Sunshine Valley, I thought I'd seen and heard the last of him, but, then, one day, to my great surprise and horror, I discovered he was also living here. Now that I'm older and have more self-esteem, I wanted to confront him and tell him how he ruined my childhood. I'd been to the Crazy Cactus a couple of times and learned that he owned the restaurant, but I never saw him. The day I went to pick up the flan, I walked back to his office. I obeyed all the rules that were posted on the door. After knocking, I heard a gruff man's voice tell me to come in. I just wanted to let him know that he'd made my life miserable when I was little, but that I was fine now. I thought, if I finally had the opportunity to stand up to him, it would make me feel better and help erase some of the negative memories I still harbored."

"But, if you just wanted to talk, why did you have to shoot him?" asked Eve.

"Believe me, I didn't go there with the intention of killing him. I simply shot him in self defense. When I first entered the office and began to speak, he glared at me and, without any hesitation, he said he knew who I was and that he was going to finish what he'd started years ago. I had said everything I'd intended to say and just wanted to get out of there, as quickly as possible. When I turned to leave, he got up from his desk and threw a heavy book at me. It hit my back and left shoulder and really hurt. In fact, my shoulder is still sore. I was stunned for a moment and stumbled into a corner, next to the door. As I stood there, trying to catch my breath, he started to come towards me with something in his hand that looked like a knife. I thought he was either going to try and rip my clothes off, or, that he was going to stab me. Fortunately, I managed to take out the hand gun that I always carry in my purse and I shot him. I just shot him to protect myself, to keep him from coming at me. I knew he wanted to hurt me, so I had to stop him. That's the reason I shot him . . . to prevent him from hurting me any further . . . or even killing me."

"But, where did you get the gun?" asked Eve.

"I've had it for many years. I found it one day on the street in Milwaukee, in front of my house. Somebody must have lost it. I was going to turn it in to the police, then decided I should keep it for my own protection. Because I'd never owned a gun before, I went to the shooting range to learn how to use it. They told me there was a silencer attached to it and that I should keep it on, so I did."

Although everything she had to say was serious, Jackie continued to explain her actions with a smile. "I was afraid of him. He was much bigger and stronger than me. When I shot him, he immediately fell down. I was so relieved. That's when I turned and was finally able to leave the office. It was a bit difficult, because the book he threw at me was blocking the door. I wasn't sure he was dead and I thought he might get up again and try to rip off my clothes or even stab me. I wanted to get away from him as quickly as possible. But, I have to tell you, when I heard that he was really dead, it was the second happiest day of my life."

Eve couldn't get over the fact that Jackie continued smiling and didn't sound the least bit remorseful, as she recounted all the events that occurred in Dick Wolf's office.

"So, that's why your shoulder was sore when we first met you at Frank's barbecue," mused Eve. "I'm curious, why didn't you tell anyone what happened?

When you came out of the office, why didn't you report what had just taken place?"

"I was scared. There were so many people in the restaurant. I was afraid they might try to hurt me too or get angry with me," replied Jackie, "so, I just walked back to the hostess, grabbed my flan, and drove back to Frank's place."

"I know you've been through quite an ordeal," remarked Adam, "but you must turn yourself in and tell the sheriff what you've just told us. If you do so, it will definitely be to your advantage. It's much better than having the authorities come to the house and pick you up. Eve and I can drive you to the station."

"I suppose you're right. It would be nice to get everything cleared up. But, I'm going on a cruise with Frank. Can we do this when I get back?" she asked, innocently.

"I'm afraid not," replied Adam. "It's already been a couple of weeks. The sooner you turn yourself in, the better. Believe me, it's for your own good and, since it was self defense, you should be okay. Also, remember, you have the right to legal representation. If you can't afford an attorney, one will be appointed by the court."

"If you don't mind a bit of advice," added Eve, "I wouldn't sound happy when you explain to the sheriff everything that happened in Dick Wolf's office." She noticed Adam looking at her sternly and shaking his head. The words "aiding" and "abetting" ran through her mind.

"Do you still have the gun?" asked Adam.

"Yes, I always keep it in my purse for protection," responded Jackie.

"Good," replied Adam, succinctly. He did his best, not to sound too alarming, as he continued. "Why don't we put it in a plastic bag and take it with us. I'm afraid you'll have to turn it over to the sheriff. In the meantime, I think we should now go and give a full report to the authorities. You can lock the front door, when we leave. You'll probably have to give the key to Sheriff Warner, so he and his men can enter, in case they need to. Most likely, they'll want the gun and they may want to search the house, as well."

Jackie went into the kitchen and returned a few seconds later, carrying a clear plastic bag. "This is for the gun" she said, as she reached into her purse.

"Here, let me help you," Adam offered quickly, before Jackie had a chance to pull out the weapon. "I think Eve should carry it." He placed the gun in the plastic bag, then handed it to his wife.

"I promise not to shoot anyone," Jackie said, with a laugh.

Adam led the way out of the house, followed by Jackie and Eve. He opened the front door of the car and suggested that Jackie sit in the passenger seat.

"Have you said anything about this to Doty and Paula, or Frank?" asked Jackie, as they began driving.

"Not a word," replied Adam. "We wanted to talk with you first."

"If I understand you correctly, you never mentioned anything about your encounter with Dick Wolf when you came back from the restaurant to Frank's house with the flan . . . why is that?" asked Eve.

"Everyone was so happy and looking forward to a nice barbecue. I didn't want to spoil their fun. I knew they'd be upset if I told them what had happened, so I just kept quiet and let them enjoy themselves."

After a short pause, Adam continued. "I want to stress that you're doing the right thing. It really is to your advantage to turn yourself in."

"I just hope it won't take too long," replied Jackie, with a sigh. "I'm supposed to have dinner with Doty, Paula, and Frank, this evening."

Eve remained silent. She couldn't get over how naïve Jackie appeared to be. She didn't seem to have the slightest clue as to the seriousness of her crime. Or, she wondered, *is this an act?* More and more, she was discovering that all was not what it appeared to be in Sunshine Valley, including the people.

When they arrived at the sheriff's station, Adam helped Jackie out of the car and led her inside. Eve followed closely behind, glad that she would soon be able to give up the gun she was carrying. Once inside, Adam asked to speak to Sheriff Warner and didn't have to wait long.

"Adam and Eve, what brings you two here? Any clues?" he asked, with a smile. "And, who's your friend? I don't believe we've met," he added, as he looked at Jackie.

Without a moment's hesitation, Jackie replied. "I'm the one who killed Dick Wolf. I'm the person you've been looking for and I've come to turn myself in."

Suddenly, a hush fell over the room.

After a short pause, Eve stepped forward and began to speak. "Miss Quinn is here, as she said, to turn herself in and she'd also like you to have her gun," explained Eve, then handed the plastic bag to Sheriff Warner.

Two officers, who'd been standing nearby and listening, immediately rushed over to the sheriff's side.

"This is serious," replied the sheriff, as he looked at the gun. After he explained her rights, Jackie declined an attorney. "Let's go into my office and you can tell me everything." He led the three of them into his office and invited them to sit at a long table. The two officers followed behind and remained standing by the door.

"Before Miss Quinn tells me what happened, why don't you explain your involvement," added Sheriff

Warner, as he looked at Adam. His voice had taken a much more serious tone.

Over the next ten minutes, Adam explained how he and Eve had come upon some information that they felt Jackie needed to hear. He then summarized the details of their discussion and her admission.

"Now," said the sheriff, as he turned to Jackie, "before I hear what you have to say, we need to take you into the back room. One of our female officers will do a quick pat down. It's a standard procedure. Then, you can come back here and tell me your side of the story."

At this moment, Jackie remained unusually low key and didn't say a word. One of the officers who was standing by the door, helped her out of her chair and led her away.

"This is going to take some time," said the sheriff, as he faced Adam. "We'll have to hold her in custody. If her story checks out, she'll be transported to the County Prosecutor's office in Tucson on Monday. She'll get a court appointed attorney, if she can't afford one. I would suggest that you both leave now, but you need to make yourselves available, if I have more questions . . . and, I'm sure I will. I really appreciate your coming in. This has been a very complex case and I hope we'll be able to close it soon."

"Please call if there's anything else you need from us. You know we want to help as much as possible," replied Adam.

Although they hated to leave, the Iversons had no choice. They both rose from the table and quietly exited.

Once they were back in their car, Eve began to speak. "This certainly has been a surprising turn of events. I still don't know what to make of it all and, I must say, Jackie doesn't seem too upset about being taken into custody. She didn't even think she needed a lawyer. I wonder what she'll have to endure in Tucson."

"Well," began Adam, "she'll definitely get a court appointed attorney and the authorities will probably give her a few tests . . . lie detector first, a mental exam, a physical exam, and I'm sure they'll test for drugs. This will be done before any bail is set. Initially, she may be charged with second degree murder. From what she told us, I believe Jackie has a good story and the prosecutor will be obliged to disprove her claim of self defense. I'm sure there are going to be quite a few interviews, especially with employees of the restaurant and his widow, of course. We may also be required to answer questions."

"I didn't realize you knew so much about the law," replied Eve, with raised eyebrows.

"You know that I've always liked watching different crime shows on television and I believe I've learned a lot from them. Actually, I did want to become a criminal lawyer when I was a young boy, but my parents talked me out of it. They said I'd encounter too many unpleasant people and situations. I listened to them and, I must say, I'm glad I did."

"We have to contact Doty, Paula, and Frank. We need to tell them what's just happened," said Eve. "They may be trying to get in touch with Jackie and could be worried, if they don't hear from her. She said they were all supposed to go out for dinner tonight."

"We can call them when we get home and ask them to come over to our house," replied Adam. "I'll call Frank and you can call Doty and Paula. I think they should all be together when we tell them this latest news."

"Another unpleasant task," sighed Eve. "I know they're going to be shocked when they hear that Jackie has confessed to murder and that she's now in jail. I'm sure they'll have a lot of questions." After a short pause, Eve continued. "I wonder if I should call George Gomez and let him know the latest developments. This is certainly going to let him off the hook."

"No, I don't think that's a good idea . . . at least, not yet. It's too soon and I wouldn't say anything, until we know more. Let's just wait a few days and see what happens in Tucson. I don't think the sheriff wants us talking about this case, at this point."

"I guess you're right, but I know George will be greatly relieved, once the word gets out," replied Eve. "He's been carrying too heavy a burden for too long."

When they arrived home, Eve placed a call to Doty and Paula, asking them to come over. She didn't provide any details, merely stated that she and Adam had something important to tell them. Adam followed suit, when he called Frank.

The three friends arrived almost simultaneously. "We're here," said Doty, cheerfully, as she entered the Iversons' house, followed by Paula and Frank. "We're anxious to hear what you want to tell us. You sounded very serious."

"Where's Jackie?" asked Frank. "I thought she might be here. I've tried calling her, but there's no answer."

Ignoring their questions, Eve began to speak in a calm voice. "Why don't you all come into the living room and sit down. We have something we need to share with the three of you."

"Is this about Jackie?" asked Paula. "Is she okay? Has she been hurt?"

When everyone was seated, Eve began to explain why she'd called them. She briefly described how she and Adam had gone over to Jackie's house to clarify some information they'd heard about her that implicated her in the murder of Dick Wolf.

"No sooner had we finished telling her what we'd learned, when she freely admitted that she was the one who killed the man, but that she'd done so in self defense," continued Eve. "She also showed us her gun and said that she always carried it in her purse for self protection," she added, after a pause.

"We convinced her that it was in her best interest to turn herself in to the sheriff," said Adam. "That's where she is now." He went on to describe, as best as he could, the procedure that would be followed.

The three friends gasped, when they heard what had transpired, and demanded to know more details. Adam explained that they were not at liberty to discuss the case, but, since they were all such good friends, he felt they had a right to know some basics.

"This can't be true," commented Doty. "Paula and I have known Jackie practically all our lives. She never even hinted that she might have killed someone. I can't believe this. It must be a mistake."

"I want to see her," said Frank, somberly. "Do you think it's possible?"

"You need to call the sheriff's station and ask if she is allowed visitors. If so, my guess is that it would only be one person at a time, but, give them a call first. Also, you should know that she's being transported to Tucson on Monday, so you might want to call today," replied Adam.

"What about our cruise to Alaska?" sighed Frank. "We're supposed to leave next week. Jackie was really looking forward to it and so was I."

"I'm afraid you're going to have to postpone the trip," replied Adam.

"We can't. The cruise line doesn't allow for last minute changes. If they keep her in jail, we won't be able to go." Frank's face had lost all color and he appeared to be on the verge of tears, as he spoke.

"I must say, this is not at all what I expected," remarked Paula. "I remember the day of Frank's barbecue, when Jackie came back from the restaurant with the flan. I don't think I'd ever seen her so happy. How is it possible that, if she just killed someone, she could be so cheerful? This has to be a mistake."

"This must be very difficult for her, but, I'm sure her law background will help her deal with this mess," observed Doty.

"What do you mean?" asked Eve. "Does Jackie have a law degree?"

"No," replied Doty. "She doesn't have a degree. When the three of us began working after high school, I became a concierge, Paula became a seamstress, and Jackie got a job in a law office as a file clerk. She must have learned a lot during those years. I'm sure that the experience she gained there will help her through this ordeal."

"Could I use your phone to call the sheriff?" asked Frank. "I really would like to talk to Jackie."

"Of course. Come with me," replied Adam, as he led his neighbor into the den.

"I think we all need to try and relax a bit," Eve commented, as she tried to comfort the two women. "This is a shock to all of us and there's nothing we can do, at this point. We have to wait and see what happens next. The only consolation we have is that Jackie has done the right thing by finally turning herself in to the authorities."

"Yes," replied Doty, "I suppose you're right, but I keep thinking about all the things we've done together lately. I never had the slightest suspicion that something was wrong. This is all so unexpected and very upsetting."

"Perhaps, during those early years, when she was so withdrawn, Jackie learned how to keep secrets," Paula suggested. "I can't seem to find any other explanation for her not saying anything to us."

After a few minutes, Adam and Frank returned to the living room.

"Well?" asked Eve. "Is it possible that Jackie can receive visitors?"

"Not today," replied Adam. "They're still interviewing her. Frank may be able to go and see her in the morning, however. But, he needs to call again before coming in, to make sure."

"I'm going to try to see her tomorrow, if possible," said Frank, somberly. "I'll let you know how she's doing and what she has to say." Looking at Paula and Doty, he continued. "Please let me know if you have any questions you'd like me to ask her, or if there's anything you want me to tell her."

"I think you could use a drink," suggested Adam, as he looked at his neighbor.

"Yes, I'd really appreciate something," replied Frank. "My nerves are a bit shattered."

"Can I get something for either of you?" asked Adam, as he turned to Doty and Paula.

"I could use a stiff drink, as well," replied Paula.

"Me too," added Doty. "I'm a bit shaky and I think a drink would help calm me."

Adam left the room and returned after a few minutes, carrying a tray with three glasses. "Help yourself. They're all the same . . . whiskey and soda. This should help relax you."

They each helped themselves, took a sip, sighed, and sat back.

Talk about Jackie and the murder continued for the next hour and involved a good deal of questions, with few answers. Finally, Frank raised himself and said he was ready to leave, and that he'd drive over to the sheriff's station in the morning. Doty and Paula followed suit, begging to be informed of any further news.

Once their neighbors exited, as was his habit when he was nervous, Adam walked over to a table, pulled out one of his pipes, and filled it with his remaining tobacco.

"I realize you're upset," said Eve, "but could you take that thing outside?"

"Just where I'm headed," replied Adam, as he walked out to the patio.

In the meantime, Eve threw herself on the living room couch and stretched her arms and legs. She was deep in thought and was glad she didn't have to talk to anyone, including her husband. She looked down at Coco, who was lying quietly on the floor, then picked her up and began to massage her.

When Adam re-entered the house, Eve looked at her husband and began to speak. "I've been going over everything that has happened and, you know what conclusion I've come to?"

"I can't wait to hear," replied Adam, as he put his pipe back in the drawer.

With Coco at her side, Eve was slow and deliberate in her delivery and chose her words carefully. "I know that you're much more knowledgeable about the law than I am, but, from everything Jackie told us, if it's true, and if she does have to go to trial, I don't think any jury would be able to come to a unanimous decision regarding her guilt or innocence."

"In other words, you think there would be a hung jury? Is that what you're implying?" asked Adam.

"I know it's still very early and we have to wait and see what all the test results reveal, especially the lie detector test, even though it's probably not one hundred percent reliable. I've heard that there are ways to get a positive result, even if someone is lying. However, based on what she told us, and, of course, if she's not holding anything back, I think a jury of twelve peers would probably believe her claim of self defense. But, there might be one or more holdouts who think she's guilty. I think it's interesting that she has some knowledge about law. Based on the way she behaved, both with us and with the sheriff, I certainly wouldn't have guessed that. Perhaps her seeming naïveté was just an act."

"You're right about one thing. It's still very early and we have to wait and see what the test results reveal. It may take a while before there's a trial, if there is one."

"I feel sorry for her friends. They all appeared very upset and hurt by the news," remarked Eve.

"Frank was really shocked," replied Adam. "So much for his cruise to Alaska. It's a shame. I think I'm going to have to spend some time with him until this matter is resolved. I'm sure he'll need quite a bit of support."

Once again, thought Eve, *another nightmare in paradise. She wondered when it would all end.*

Chapter 11

Jackie's confession and subsequent arrest deeply affected all of her friends. When Frank went to the sheriff's station to see her on the day following her arrest, he was only allowed a short fifteen minute visit. He was told that, due to the seriousness of the alleged crime and her right to a speedy trial, she was being transported to Tucson sooner than expected. When he returned home, he reported that Jackie appeared to be in good shape and didn't seem upset by what was occurring.

Both Adam and Eve, however, were overwhelmed by everything they'd heard and experienced. Consequently, they had difficulty resuming their normal activities for the next several days. On Tuesday morning, once again, they made their way out to the patio, each carrying a cup of coffee and a newspaper.

"I know I should try to do some swimming," said Eve, "but I can't bear going to the pool this soon. I'm sure I'd run into Peggy Walsh and, no doubt, she'd ask me where Jackie was. I don't want to have to lie, or deal with any questions about her . . . not at this point."

"Same here," replied Adam. "I don't want to go to the gym yet, in case I run into that man who told me about the red dress."

"I don't even feel like painting," added Eve. "I just want to sit here quietly, drink my coffee, and do my crosswords. They're usually a good distraction. I really need to try to get my mind off of Jackie's confession."

After a few minutes of filling in her puzzle, Eve glanced over at Adam. "See if you can answer this one," she said. "The clue is 'out of the can.' The answer has two words and nine letters."

Adam looked blankly at Eve. "In the bowl?" he asked.

"Nope. That's three words. The answer is 'free again.' Even doing the crossword puzzle won't allow me to escape from thinking about Jackie's predicament. I wonder if she'll ever be free again."

"Now that she's in Tucson, she has a court appointed attorney. Frank drove there this morning. He's been very supportive. He told me that he was also going to post bail for her. So, she may be free again, at least temporarily. He should be back soon . . . with Jackie."

Eve continued doing her puzzle, while Adam scanned the newspaper.

"You're not going to believe this," he said, as he waved the paper at his wife. "Take a look. It's Jackie's mug shot and a short report about her confession and arrest."

Eve took the newspaper from Adam and slowly read through the account. "I'm surprised this appeared so quickly. It doesn't really say much, just that she admitted killing Dick Wolf and is claiming self defense. It doesn't say anything that we don't already know. At least, she looks a bit more serious and isn't smiling in her photograph."

"I think she was probably told to look straight ahead and not smile," replied Adam. "I'm sure she'll have quite a bit to say when she and Frank get back."

"Now, for sure, I don't want to go to the pool today," said Eve. "No doubt Peggy Walsh and others are aware of this latest news and will hound me with questions. Thank goodness we're not mentioned in the article, but I know how quickly word gets around here."

Suddenly, Coco sprang to her feet and ran inside, barking.

"Maybe that's them now," said Adam. "I'll get it."

It didn't take long for Adam to return, followed, not by Frank and Jackie, but by Doty and Paula.

Doty was waving the paper. "Did you see this? Did you see the story about Jackie?"

"Yes," replied Eve. "We just read it, but there's nothing new in it. We're waiting for Frank to return. He went to Tucson to post bail for Jackie and they should be here shortly."

"We know. We tried calling each of them, but no answer," said Doty, breathlessly. "We thought they might be here."

"Not yet. Why don't you both sit down and wait until they arrive," suggested Eve. "Would either of you like something to drink? We're just having some coffee."

Both women shook their heads, declining the offer.

"Maybe later," said Paula. "Right now, I'm just anxious to see Jackie and hear what she has to say. We're both so concerned for her. I'm sure this has been a very upsetting experience, but I hope she's okay."

The four friends sat back in their chairs, patiently awaiting the arrival of Frank and Jackie, and exchanging opinions as to what might happen next. As they were talking, Eve glanced over the patio wall and spotted Frank. She rose from the chair and waved for him to come and join them.

When he entered the Iversons' patio, everyone simultaneously blurted out the same question. "Where's Jackie?"

"Did she come back with you?" asked Paula. "We're anxious to know how she's doing."

Frank had a very sad look on his face, as he replied. "I'm afraid it's not good news." His voice was very somber.

"Pull up a chair and tell us what happened," said Adam.

Frank appeared unsteady and sat down slowly. Eve noticed that his hands were shaking, as he began to speak. "Well, as I promised, I went to Tucson to post bail for Jackie. I met with her attorney and I have to say, I liked him. He's very supportive. However, Jackie has been charged with second degree murder and there's a very tough prosecutor. They did a search of her background and he claims that, because she has family in Mexico, she's now considered a flight risk. Even though she maintained that she had no intention of leaving the country, the judge agreed with the prosecutor and her bail has been denied. Sadly, she has to remain in custody until there's a trial. This could take weeks, even months. I find it all very discouraging."

"Did you see her?" asked Doty, as she gasped for air.

"I only saw her briefly. I must say, I think she's holding up better than her friends. She didn't seem the least bit upset and said she was being treated very well. She had no complaints."

"What about tests?" asked Adam. "Did you get any news about possible results?"

"Her attorney told me she passed the lie detector test and that several other tests would be administered this week . . . I'm not sure which ones. He also told me that a lot of interviews were going to be conducted . . . Dick Wolf's widow, for one, as well as all current and former employees at the restaurant. I'm afraid it's really going to take quite some time before things get resolved. I still can't get over what's happened. We were supposed to leave on Thursday for our cruise." After a short pause, he looked at Adam. "Would you and Eve like to have our tickets?" he asked, half-heartedly.

"That's very kind of you, Frank," replied Adam, somberly. "I know you mean well, but, given the short notice and under the circumstances, we couldn't possibly accept your offer. Besides, I think we all need to be here to support each other during this difficult time."

"Absolutely," added Eve. "We couldn't possibly leave you alone now. We all have to stick together. And, let me emphasize, if one of you needs to talk during the coming weeks, please don't hesitate to call or to come over. Both Adam and I want to be as helpful as possible. Who knows, perhaps this will end sooner than we realize. After all, as you said, Jackie passed the lie detector test and, even though it can't be used in court, it certainly works in her favor."

"I'm still perplexed," remarked Paula. "I thought we were such good friends and it's difficult to comprehend why Jackie never said anything to Doty and me about the murder . . . not even a hint. She never even mentioned that she owned a gun."

"She probably didn't want to upset you," responded Eve, although she wasn't certain her words rang true.

After discussing Jackie's current situation and potential future for another hour, Doty, Paula, and Frank opted to leave the Iversons. Each of them expressed a need to be quiet.

"Let me repeat," said Eve. "Don't any of you hesitate to call us or come over if you have questions, or simply just want to talk. Remember, we're always here for you."

Once they all left, Eve turned to Adam and began to speak. "I'm really surprised that Jackie was denied bail. I wonder how good a lawyer she has."

"I'm not certain, but the denial might have something to do with the fact that she didn't immediately turn herself in. Even though, on the surface, her story might seem plausible, the fact that she waited so long works against her."

"You may be right," responded Eve, then changed the subject. "Now, I have to go to the restaurant and see Valerie and George. I'm sure they've read the latest news and, no doubt, will have questions. I need to explain a few things. I owe it to them and, now that Jackie's confession and arrest have been made public, I want to express my support for George. I'm sure this is a huge relief for him."

"I thought you might want to talk with them," remarked Adam. "Go ahead. Coco and I will be here, just waiting for you."

Eve went into the house, changed her clothes, then got into the car, and headed for the restaurant. Once she began driving, she rehearsed in her mind how much information she should share with her new friends.

When she arrived at the Sunshine Flower, she scanned the parking lot to make sure it was safe and, once again, was relieved to see that it was empty. Upon entering the restaurant, she saw no one. "Valerie?" she called out. "George? Is anyone here?"

"Oh, Eve," said Valerie, as she emerged from the back of the restaurant. "I was going to call you. Donna, George, and I have just been reading the newspaper. We're back here in the banquet room. Why don't you join us."

Eve followed Valerie and was greeted by George and Donna, who were sitting at the table, both smiling broadly.

"I'm so glad you're here," said George. "Did you see the paper? I can't believe the good news. It's incredible. I'm finally off the hook. They have the real killer of

Dick Wolf in custody. Now, I won't have to keep denying my guilt to everyone. My wife and children are going to be so relieved."

"Yes, George. I'm so pleased for you," replied Eve. Although she was genuinely happy for George Gomez, her feelings were somewhat mixed. She felt badly that the killer was someone she'd come to know and like.

"I know you had something to do with this woman's confession," said Valerie, coyly. "Based on what I told you about Dick's childhood, you guessed who I was talking about. Why didn't you tell me that you knew this woman and what you suspected?"

"I wasn't absolutely certain you were talking about Jackie Quinn and had to make sure, before I said anything. I would have come here sooner, believe me, but the sheriff warned me and Adam not to say anything until the official word was out. Now that the confession and arrest have been made public, I feel a bit freer to talk." Eve was very apologetic. She explained how she'd come to know Jackie Quinn and began to describe the series of events that led up to her confession and subsequent arrest.

"I understand that she's claiming self defense, but I'm not so sure it wasn't deliberate," remarked Valerie. "I knew this man and all the terrible things he was capable of doing. Believe me, if someone had treated me the way his mother told me he treated this woman as a child, I would have wanted to kill him, as well. I certainly wouldn't have waited such a long time to do it, either. I'm quite certain there are many others who share my feelings."

"Well," added Eve "from what I gather, even though it's not admissible in court, she did pass the lie detector test. At this point, I think we should give her the benefit of the doubt and believe her claim of self-defense, unless evidence emerges to indicate that the murder was deliberate and pre-meditated."

"One good thing for us," began Donna, "at least the killer isn't connected to the restaurant. I was afraid he or she might be a current or former employee and it would not be good for business. We've seen some cars driving by here, slowly. I'm always afraid the men who came after George might want to hurt us, as well. Maybe, now, they'll go away."

"Let's hope so," added Valerie. "I know some folks around here believe that I killed my husband to inherit his money. This woman's confession lets me and everyone else off the hook. However, we did get a call from the prosecutor's office this morning. They want to interview me, Donna, and George, as well as all the employees who were here the day Dick was killed. They also want to talk with employees who were fired, or who quit on their own. I'm afraid we're going to have to postpone our opening for a few more weeks, but it's worth it."

"It looks like our women today are following tradition," said Donna. "By opening the restaurant, Valerie is following in the footsteps of the early female entrepreneurs and Jackie Quinn is our current gun slinger. When I write my book . . . or article, I wonder if I should bring it up to date and include their stories."

"I think it would probably be of greater interest and value to simply concentrate on the early women pioneers," remarked Eve.

"You're probably right," responded Donna. "People can get information about today's women from current articles in newspapers and magazines. They usually don't know much about the past. I'll stick to my original plan and keep a focus that's historical."

Well, reflected Eve, *the mood here is certainly more upbeat than what she had just experienced at home.* As they kept talking, she realized that Valerie and Donna have been much more concerned about the identity of the killer than they'd been willing to openly admit. Perhaps they had their own suspicions, but were reluctant acknowledge them. In any case, she thought they seemed extremely relieved at hearing about Jackie's confession and arrest.

"I wonder how many years this woman will get," mused George. "I think they should let her go free. I'll bet anything she killed the Wolf in self-defense, as she claims. He threatened to hurt me several times and I know others have had similar experiences. If I'd had a gun when he came at me, I probably would have shot him too. He was a very mean man and deserved what happened to him. I hope she gets off. What do you think, Donna?"

"I'm not sure. I know you're right. He did threaten a lot of people, but, It could go either way. I don't really have enough information to make an informed assessment. We'll just have to wait and see what develops."

"Yes," replied Eve. "I think this is going to be a difficult case for the prosecutor and let's try not to jump to any conclusions. I'm sure a lot of opinions will begin floating around, but I think we should try to avoid adding to the gossip."

Eve thought she'd said enough and was eager to leave. She'd made her apologies and reported everything she felt appropriate, at this time.

"Thank you for stopping by," said Valerie. "Please let us know if you hear any late-breaking news. I feel sorry for this woman, but I'm glad we're headed towards a resolution."

On her way home, Eve wasn't as disturbed as she had anticipated she might be. She was happy for George, but still somewhat concerned about Jackie.

Nevertheless, even though she couldn't explain her reasoning, she had a strong gut instinct that, in the long run, the woman would emerge intact from her predicament.

Chapter 12

As expected, Adam and Eve were asked to come to the sheriff's station to be interviewed by both prosecuting and defense attorneys regarding their involvement with Jackie Quinn. The session was short and uneventful. Once again, they explained what they'd discussed with their friend before she turned herself in to the sheriff. They repeatedly stated that they had no knowledge of any pre-meditation and they agreed to provide testimony in court for the defense, if required.

Following their interrogation, the Iversons returned to the sanctity of their home. Time passed without any disturbing news from the outside world. Nevertheless, Adam and Eve had little desire to appear in public. They were both reluctant to discuss anything related to Jackie Quinn's arrest with nosy neighbors.

Finally, after several weeks, Eve's distress began to recede. One sunny day, as she found herself, once again, sitting on the patio, she suddenly threw down her newspaper. "I've had it," she blurted out to Adam, who was seated next to her. "Word games at night . . . crossword puzzles during the day. I haven't had any exercise in ages and I haven't even done any painting. I'm tired of just sitting here and vegetating. To start with, I think I'm going to risk going for a dip in the pool. I'm sure I'll run into Peggy Walsh, but it can't be helped. I want to get back to something resembling a normal life."

"I guess you're right," responded Adam. "I'm almost getting used to doing nothing, but I know it's not good for me. Not today, but tomorrow, I plan to return to the gym. I think you should go to the pool and just focus on doing your laps. I may go across and visit with Frank later, when he returns from Tucson. Jackie's confession and arrest have affected him deeply. I've noticed that he's starting to withdraw again and he needs whatever support I can offer."

Eve pushed herself out of her chair with some difficulty. Every move she made seemed more strenuous than usual. "We really need to get that exercycle," she said, as she slowly got up and went into the house to prepare for her swim.

As she headed out, Eve had more difficulty walking than usual. Although the pavement was dry, due to her stiffness, it took her a little longer to reach the pool. Once she arrived, she was glad to see that it was relatively empty. She was especially relieved to see that Peggy Walsh wasn't sitting in her usual spot.

After she placed her bag and robe on an empty chair, Eve walked over to the edge of the pool, removed her slippers, then slid into the water. She slowly began swimming up and down one of the long lanes. As she finished her tenth and last lap, she heard a woman calling her name. She looked up and, as she'd anticipated, there was Peggy Walsh, waving at her.

"Eve," Peggy called out, "I haven't seen you in ages. You must come and talk to me when you're finished swimming."

Eve took her time leaving the pool. She wasn't particularly eager to talk to Peggy, but knew it was unavoidable.

"Where have you been?" asked Peggy. "I was going to call you. I thought maybe you were ill or had left town, for some reason."

Eve made an enormous effort to conceal her reluctance to engage in conversation. "I've just been doing a little hang gliding, golf, and horseback riding," she replied, with a laugh.

"I'll bet. I've missed you."

"I've been very busy doing things around the house."

"I wanted to talk to you about Jackie Quinn. I saw how she confessed to the murder of Dick Wolf. It's been in all the newspapers and on television. But, I have to tell you, I wasn't surprised when I first heard the news."

"Oh, why is that?" Eve asked in a flat voice, as she continued drying herself.

"Well, I was here one day when she was swimming. This was a while ago. You weren't here that day. All of a sudden, I heard her yell out to someone else who crossed in front of her, 'You better watch out or you'll be sorry'."

"That's not very unusual," remarked Eve, casually. "Serious swimmers like to use the long lanes and they get annoyed when someone splashes across the pool in front of them. It breaks their momentum. I know, because it's happened to me a few times. You'll see what I mean, once you learn how to swim."

"Yes, I can understand that, but you should have heard the tone of her voice. It wasn't the same sweet, happy-go-lucky woman you introduced me to. Believe me, I saw another side to her that day. She didn't even recognize me or say hello. So, when I read that she admitted to being the killer of Dick Wolf, I wasn't at all surprised. I began thinking and wondered if she might also have brought a gun with her to the pool."

"I wouldn't get too carried away. So far, all we know is that, even though she admitted the killing, she's claiming self-defense and, right now, we have to go with that. We need to just sit back quietly and see what happens." Eve was reluctant to discuss anything further concerning Jackie and prepared to return home.

"Do you know if she passed the lie detector test? Were there any other tests? Has a trial date been set yet?" Peggy didn't let up on her desire for more information.

"I just know what I read in the paper . . . same as you. I'm sure we'll learn more as the days pass. But, now, if you'll excuse me, I must be going. I really needed a good swim and, I assure you, I'll be back again soon." Eve finished drying herself, pulled on her robe and turned to leave.

"Let me know if you hear anything new," Peggy called after Eve.

Once she arrived back home and finished showering, Eve went out to the patio to hang up her bathing suit and robe. She spotted Adam across the way. He seemed to be involved in an animated conversation with Frank, who was waving his arms in the air. *I hope that's a good sign*, she thought, then sat down by her easel and waited for her husband to return.

As she began drawing on her sketch pad, Eve looked up and noticed Adam leaving their neighbor and heading for home.

"Well, I'm almost afraid of this question, but, how was the pool?" he asked, as he opened the patio gate. "I hope you didn't have to go through too deep an interrogation."

"No, it wasn't too bad," replied Eve.

As Adam sat down, Eve rose from her easel and pulled up a chair next to her husband, then began to relate what Peggy Walsh had told her about the comment Jackie had made to a fellow swimmer. "It's funny," she said, "when Peggy told me what she'd heard her say, I found myself defending Jackie. I also get annoyed if someone crosses in front of me, when I'm doing my laps."

"It doesn't sound too serious," said Adam. "Now, if you think you're ready, I have quite a bit of news that you might want to hear."

"I thought as much. You were at Frank's place for some time. I'm anxious to hear what you learned. Has a trial date been set yet?"

"No, just the opposite," began Adam. "There isn't going to be a trial. I'm pleased to report that the case against Jackie has been dismissed."

"You're kidding! Are you serious?" asked Eve, in disbelief.

"Yes. Frank had quite a bit of late-breaking news to share with me. Apparently, after all the tests and interviews with about thirty people, the prosecutor felt there wasn't enough conclusive evidence to disprove Jackie's claim of self-defense. First of all, her gun tested positive, so it's clear that she was the one who shot Dick Wolf. However, as you know, she passed the lie detector test. They also did a physical and found some residual soft tissue damage on her shoulder, where she claimed he hit her with that book. They did a mental health test and also tested for drugs. It seems that she's taking some prescribed mood elevators . . . just as I suspected. However, they're mild and she doesn't appear to be overdoing anything. They also searched her house and only found a two weeks' supply . . . prescribed by a doctor in Milwaukee. That's not much and they didn't find any illicit drugs in her system, thank goodness. As for the people who were interviewed, so many of them claimed that Dick Wolf had physically threatened them and, even though no charges were ever brought against him, numerous complaints were made to the sheriff by former employees. They pretty much supported Jackie's allegation. So, bottom line is, there isn't enough solid evidence to warrant a trial. She's going to be released tomorrow. Frank will bring her home."

Eve sat quietly, stunned by what she was hearing. "That's quite a story. I thought that, if she did have to go to trial, there could be a hung jury. This is even better. I'll bet Frank is happy to hear the news."

"Yes, but he does have some reservations. He believes that Jackie killed the man in self-defense, as she claims. However, he's concerned that she was able to relate so positively to him and to Doty and Paula, knowing what she'd done. She never seemed the least bit upset about anything. She certainly never gave the impression that she'd killed a man. He wishes that she had shared something with him about her encounter with Dick Wolf at the restaurant. Also, he's not particularly thrilled to hear that she's on uppers and that she always carried a gun with her."

"I can't say I blame him," replied Eve. "I also find the gun a bit disconcerting."

"It certainly would have been easier on all of her friends if she'd shared what she'd done and what she was going through," added Adam, thoughtfully. "But, then, as my mother always told me, nobody's perfect."

"My mother told me the same thing, but, I don't think either of our mothers had murder in mind."

"Somehow, I sense that you're not especially pleased with the outcome of this mess. I thought you supported Jackie. Don't you think her claim of self-defense is true? Do you think her action was pre-meditated?"

"Actually, I have rather mixed feelings," replied Eve, with some hesitation. "I'm glad the case is coming to an end, but I keep remembering what Doty said about Jackie's job in a law office. Perhaps she learned how to plan a murder and cover it up, to make it look like self-defense. For someone who apparently has a legal background, even though she was only a file clerk, she seemed incredibly ignorant when we first talked with her. Perhaps I'm too suspicious, but, in my humble opinion, it just doesn't make sense."

"As you said before," interjected Adam, "if this case were to go to trial, you thought there would be a hung jury. Well, we seem to have one right here in our own home. Based on the lack of concrete evidence to indicate otherwise, I'm inclined to believe Jackie's self-defense claim, but you appear to have some doubts. Again, my vote is based on the evidence, or lack thereof, but I fear yours is based solely on conjecture and intuition."

"Yes, I know. Nevertheless, I believe that, underneath, Jackie is much smarter than she might appear to be in public," countered Eve. "On the surface, she comes across as being somewhat naïve, but I think there's another side to her. I think she's much smarter than her seemingly innocent posturing. Everybody, including Jackie, knew what Dick Wolf was like and that it wouldn't take much to get him riled up. She could have gone to his office and purposely said something to get him angry. Then, when he came towards her, she could have simply pulled out her gun and shot him. In other words, she would have been prepared."

"That's a possibility," replied Adam, "but, once again, there's no proof to substantiate your view. It's pure conjecture and would never hold up in court."

"I know that. I'm just letting you know my own personal take on things," countered Eve. "I'm also surprised that she had such perfect aim, considering how rattled she claimed to be. Her one bullet went right into his heart."

As they continued exchanging opinions, Eve heard the phone ring inside the house. "I'll get it," she said. "It could be Doty."

After a few minutes, Eve returned to the patio, carrying her bag. "That was Valerie. She wants me to come to the restaurant right away. She said she has a nice surprise for me and it's very important that I come immediately. I don't think it has anything to do with Jackie and I'm sure it won't take long."

"She's really becoming dependent on you. Go ahead. I'm just going to sit here and mull over everything Frank told me."

As Eve drove to the restaurant, she tried to sort out the news she'd just heard. She wasn't prepared to discuss anything unpleasant and hoped that Valerie's request to see her didn't have anything to do with Jackie. As she pulled into the parking lot, she was surprised to see more cars than usual. Upon entering the restaurant, she spotted several employees who were busy rearranging tables.

"Over here, Eve," called Valerie. She was standing next to Donna and a man with a camera. "I'm so glad you could make it. You're just in time."

"In time for what?" asked Eve, blankly.

"Well, this gentleman is from the *Sunshine Valley Times*," replied Valerie, as she pointed to the man standing next to her. "He wants to take a photograph of you, Donna, and me, standing in front of your painting."

This announcement was not at all what Eve had anticipated and she wasn't particularly keen on having her picture taken at this time. Nevertheless, she felt there was no way out, and, so, she reluctantly agreed to the request.

"I did an interview this morning about the re-opening of the restaurant," Valerie began to explain.

"The reporter really liked your painting and thought it would be nice to include a photograph with the story. So, here we are."

"Okay," said the photographer, "why don't the three of you line up by the side of the painting. Eve . . . I think you should stand in the middle."

The three women did as they were told, trying not to block the canvas.

"Very good," said the man, as he began snapping the camera. "That'll do it. The story will probably run in the paper day after tomorrow and we'll include one photo." He thanked the women, then turned and quickly exited the restaurant.

"This was certainly unexpected, but, I wish you would have warned me," Eve said to Valerie.

"I wanted to surprise you. I love it . . . both you and your painting will be in the paper. You deserve all the recognition you can get."

"Yes, you do," echoed Donna. "I can't wait to read the story and see our picture."

"Thank you," replied Eve. "So, do you now have an idea as to when you'll be able to open the restaurant?"

"Yes, thank goodness . . . in a week," answered a smiling Valerie. "All the interviews are finished and am I glad. I was interviewed for over two hours. I told the attorneys what I told you. I didn't have any knowledge as to whether Jackie Quinn planned to kill Dick, or if it was self-defense. I told them how mean he was and that, even though he never actually hit me, he threatened to do so many times. Finally, I was able to leave and was told that I might be asked to testify in court when, and if, there's a trial. I hope that never happens."

Eve wasn't certain whether or not to tell Valerie what she'd just learned about the trial, then decided it would help ease her friend's mind, if she shared some of her knowledge.

"I don't think you need to worry. I just learned that there won't be a trial. There isn't enough hard evidence to disprove Jackie's claim of self-defense and the case has been dismissed." Eve thought her response was clean and simple and hoped it would satisfy Valerie.

"Are you serious? How wonderful! I was so afraid that I'd have to go to court. We need to celebrate. I can't wait to tell George. I think this outcome will please everybody. Thank you for sharing the good news."

"Now, I'm off," said Eve, before Valerie could begin questioning her. "I'm looking forward to some fine dining at the Sunshine Flower restaurant."

"Remember, you and Adam will be our guests . . . and be sure to bring any friends you might want to invite, as well. I'll call you and let you know when we open. Thank you again for the wonderful news. I know George and Donna will be very happy, when I tell them."

As Eve returned to her car and began driving, the solitude of the desert enabled her to collect her thoughts. Although she and Adam had only been living in Sunshine Valley for less than a year, so many unexpected events had occurred during that time . . . both good and bad. In all her years of teaching, she always felt that she had control over her life. Now, she felt like an innocent and helpless bystander. One thing she could control was what she told Adam and she decided not to tell him about the photograph. She wanted to see the look of surprise on his face when he opened the newspaper.

Chapter 13

At four-thirty, the following afternoon, having finished some heavy shopping, Eve found herself stretched out on the living room couch, scanning through some art magazines that she'd been collecting for the past few months. All of a sudden, Adam came rushing in from the patio.

"Well, she's free and home again," he said, smiling. "I just saw Frank and he brought Jackie back to paradise."

"'Wonderful. He must be relieved," replied Eve. "Did Doty and Paula go with him?"

"No. He went alone. He drove Jackie back to her own home. She wanted to get back to her familiar surroundings and said she needed to color her hair."

"They probably don't provide hair color in jail," replied Eve, with a laugh. "But, I'm not terribly surprised that Doty and Paula didn't go with Frank. I think they're both a bit disappointed in their long-time friend, especially Paula. I know I would be."

"Perhaps. Anyway, Frank invited us to his place tomorrow afternoon for a little welcome home celebration . . . no big deal, just some drinks and a few appetizers. I accepted for both of us. Doty and Paula will be there, as well."

"Good thing I went shopping. We can bring some chips and a dip. It'll be interesting to see how Jackie looks and acts. I wonder if her time in jail has changed her. I'm pleased she's home again, but I don't want to hear any more gory details about the murder."

"I doubt that Jackie wants to talk about the murder or anything else unpleasant. Frank said she sounds very positive and is looking forward to continuing the wonderful life she started here. I think we all need to put the past behind us now and let bygones be bygones."

"That may be easier said than done," replied Eve. "I'm sure word has already gotten out about her release. I guarantee she's going to be the center of attention for many locals. I know the pool will be filled with folks wanting to see the latest Sunshine Valley celebrity and hear what she has to say. I think it'll be quite a while before things settle down."

Although she continued flipping through her art magazine, Eve couldn't help thinking about Jackie. Because she still had so many mixed feelings regarding the woman's plea and subsequent release from jail, she felt she'd have to choose her words very carefully, when the group of friends got together.

During the night, a gentle rain began to fall on the desert. Although, by sunrise, the sun was trying to poke its way through the clouds, Adam and Eve chose to have their breakfast in the kitchen, since their patio was still wet.

As they were seated opposite each other at the table, Adam picked up the newspaper. "I can't believe this picture," he blurted out.

"How do I look?" asked Eve, thinking he was referring to her.

"You look fine. Why? Are you going out?"

"No . . . How do I look in the picture?"

Adam stared at his wife, not comprehending her question. "This isn't you. It's Jackie. It's a photograph of her leaving jail. Here . . . see for yourself," he said, then handed the paper to Eve.

Much to Eve's surprise, there was a large photograph of Jackie on the front page. She was smiling and waving, as she was about to get into a car. The headline read *Killer Set Free*. She continued to read through the story that described how Jackie had initially been charged with second-degree murder. However, because she claimed she killed Dick Wolf in self-defense and, because the prosecuting attorneys couldn't uncover any evidence to repudiate her claim, the case was dismissed and her record cleared. Nevertheless, should new evidence emerge, the case could always be re-opened in the future.

"This doesn't look like the same woman we know," remarked Eve, after she finished reading the article. "She looks so different . . . gray hair . . . no makeup. I can see why she wanted to quickly get back to her own home and take care of herself."

"Well, for sure, there's no doubt now that she'll become a local celebrity," added Adam. "Not many folks around here get to have their picture in the newspaper and, certainly, not on the front page."

Eve handed the paper back to Adam. He reread the article, then continued turning the pages. "Oh, no—" he blurted out again. "I can't believe this. There's also a picture of you in the paper. You didn't tell me you had your picture taken. What do you know? You and Jackie are both celebrities. Take a look." Once again, he handed the paper back to his wife.

"This isn't bad," she said, as she looked at her photograph, then scanned the account about the opening of the Sunshine Flower restaurant. "I wanted to surprise you. That's why I didn't say anything. I just wish they didn't have to run both stories on the same day."

"How about that! My wife is a famous artist and she has a friend who's a freed killer," retorted Adam, sardonically.

"Stop," Eve snapped. "I don't want any more grief. Unfortunately, my new art career has also taken me to some places I'd rather not go. If my one painting hadn't been stolen, we wouldn't have seen it in the restaurant and we wouldn't have discovered Dick Wolf's body. I wouldn't have met his widow, who provided information that led to identifying Jackie as the killer, and I wouldn't have my picture in the paper on the same day as hers."

"But, some good things have also occurred," Adam reminded his wife. "You had a wonderful one-woman exhibit at the Sunshine Gallery and sold quite a few paintings. You were also commissioned to do this painting," he added, as he pointed to the photograph in the paper. "Jack Slater is going to love this, as will your admirers. I think you should start looking on the bright side of things. We need to move forward. The worst is over."

"I certainly hope you're right, but, I can't wait to get our little welcome home party behind us. What I want, more than anything, is to start painting again and get my mind off Jackie. She's taken up way too much of my mental energy."

Once they finished eating, Adam looked down at Coco, who'd started to make circles around his legs. "I know, Coco, it's time. You're ready to go for your walk. We're going now," he said, as he got up and secured the dog's leash.

"You don't think it's too wet to go for a walk?" asked Eve.

"I think it's dry enough by now. We can always jump over the puddles, if we have to."

As Adam and Coco left the house, Eve cleared the breakfast dishes. The only interruption was a phone call from Valerie, inviting Adam and Eve to the re-opening of the restaurant on the following Saturday. "Be sure to invite your friends, as well," she told Eve. "Don't forget to include Jackie Quinn. I want to meet her and so do Donna and George."

Although she wasn't particularly thrilled with the invitation, Eve graciously accepted it and complimented Valerie on the newspaper article and photograph.

When Adam returned from his walk with Coco, he spotted Eve, who was lying on the couch, looking through the newspaper. "I have to go out again, but I won't be long," he said to his wife.

"Now what?" asked Eve, as she looked up. "You were just out. Where are you going this time?"

"I can't tell you, but I'll be right back," Adam replied.

"All these secrets . . . I think you've been influenced too much by Jackie," chided Eve.

Without saying another word, Adam made a quick exit and got into his car. As promised, he was only gone about fifteen minutes.

"I told you'd I'd be right back," he said to Eve, as he re-entered the house. "Now, I have a very nice surprise for you. I want you to come out to the patio with me. Don't worry . . . it's dry now."

"I can't imagine what you've been up to this time," responded Eve, as she got up from the couch and followed her husband out to the patio.

"Sit down. I'll be right back," said Adam, as he left his wife and walked to his car.

It didn't take long for Adam to return. This time, he was pushing an exercycle onto the patio.

"What? What's this?" gasped Eve.

"It's an exercycle . . . something you've been wanting," replied her husband.

"But, where did you get it?"

"Well, when I was out walking Coco, I ran into a man who's just purchased a home . . . about two blocks from here. We began talking and he asked me if I knew anyone who might want an exercycle. He said it was in the house when he bought it and he won't be using it. He just wanted to get rid of it. So, I let him know I was interested. How do you like that?"

"What a coincidence! It doesn't look as if anyone has used it. This will be perfect for us," said Eve, as she began inspecting the bike. "Let's put it over there, by the wall. I think the roof will protect it from rain."

Adam rolled the exercycle over to the side of the house and stepped back. "There. We're really going to enjoy this."

"I think Coco is going to love it too," replied Eve, as the dog ran around in circles and began barking.

"Let's try it out," said Adam. "You go first."

As directed, Eve climbed up on the exercycle and began pedaling. "It even has a timer on it," she exclaimed. "This is just what I had in mind. How much did the man want for it?"

"Nothing. I offered to pay him, but he wouldn't accept anything. He was just anxious to get it out of the house," replied Adam.

"Unbelievable You really found a winner," said Eve, with a smile, as she continued pedaling. "Can't we just stay here this afternoon?"

"Don't worry. You'll have plenty of time to get all the exercise you want."

Around three o'clock, when they both finished taking turns on their new exercycle, Adam and Eve prepared to go over to Frank's house. After putting their appetizers and a bottle of wine in a bag, Eve followed her husband to the patio door. They both looked out, then hesitated for a moment, before exiting.

"Although the ground is dry, I'm worried that it might start raining again," said Eve. "I think we should leave Coco at home. We won't be gone very long . . . I guarantee it." She leaned over, petted the dog on her head, then followed her husband out the door.

"Even if it doesn't rain any more, I think we'll probably be celebrating indoors," remarked Adam.

After crunching their way across the gravel path, they heard laughter coming from inside Frank's house.

"It sounds like Jackie's already here," said Eve.

Once they entered the patio and walked up to the open back door, the Iversons were greeted by their four friends. Eve couldn't believe her eyes. There was Jackie, wearing her favorite red dress, looking better than ever. Her jet black curly hair surrounded a smiling, happy face.

"Come on in," said Frank. "We're so pleased that we're finally able to have this little celebration. It's not much, but the main thing is that Jackie's now a free woman and back home, where she belongs."

"Yes," exclaimed Jackie. "I'm so happy to be here. After six long weeks, the three musketeers are together again."

As Eve scanned the room, she noticed that Paula, who was sitting alone in a corner, was the only one not smiling. She then handed her bag to Doty, who took it and went into the kitchen.

"I'm so glad you're here," added Jackie, as she walked over to the Iversons and hugged each of them. "I have to thank both of you. If I hadn't listened to you, I wouldn't be here now . . . and a free woman."

"Both Adam and I were so happy for you, when we heard the news," remarked Eve. "I know it probably wasn't easy for you, but jail doesn't seem to have done you much harm. You're looking very good."

Remember, she chided herself, *choose your words carefully.*

"It wasn't too bad, but the accommodations weren't exactly first-class. The bed was small and hard. It was difficult to bathe and I wasn't able to color my hair, or put on any makeup. I hardly ate anything. There weren't any barbecues or piano concerts. The good part is, I lost a little weight. You wouldn't believe all the questions I was asked . . . the same ones, over and over. They checked my background, both here and in Milwaukee, but I have a clean record. I've never even had so much as a parking ticket. Actually, there were moments when I feared I'd never get out, especially when I was denied bail. I thought they'd just lock me up and throw away the key. But, I had a very good lawyer and, in the end, I think they believed what I told them and finally, they had to let me go free. I'm very pleased to say that my record is clean again."

"That's wonderful," said Eve. "Now, you can get back to making a nice life for yourself here in Sunshine Valley."

"Yes, but, I'm afraid people aren't going to leave me alone. There were a few neighbors milling around in front of my house this morning. I even noticed a couple of cars driving back and forth. I'm sure that, when I go to the pool again, I'll be hit with all sorts of questions."

"You may be the center of attention for a while. That's only normal, considering the circumstances. But, I think everything will soon quiet down. A lot of part-time residents are starting to leave for the summer. I'm certain that, by fall, people will be getting on with their own lives and leave you alone. I've noticed that, when something unusual happens, people get excited at first, but, they also tend to have short memories."

"I hope you're right," replied Jackie. "I really don't like talking about myself, especially if it's something negative. That's why I never told my friends here what happened. Everyone was so happy and I didn't want to stir things up and upset them."

Once again, Eve looked over at Paula, who remained expressionless.

"I think the worst part about being in jail is that I didn't get to go on the cruise with Frank," continued Jackie. "I was really looking forward to it. I hope we can do it some time in the future."

Ignoring any reference to the cruise, Frank began to speak. "Let's all have a drink and some appetizers," he said, waving his arms. "We're so happy to have Jackie back with us again."

Just as he finished, Doty emerged from the kitchen, carrying a tray filled with appetizers and placed them around the dining room table.

"Now, please sit down," added Frank. "We want to toast our friend Jackie and let her know how glad we are that she's back home again."

As directed, each person took a seat at the table, including Paula, who was the last to join the group. When everyone was in place, Frank stood up and poured some wine into the glasses. "To Jackie. Welcome home," he said, simply, as he raised his glass.

"Welcome home," added everyone, including Paula, as they each lifted a glass.

Although Jackie sported her usual cheerful demeanor, Eve couldn't help noticing how subdued Doty, Paula, and Frank appeared to be, compared to previous gatherings. She wondered if, perhaps, they shared her mixed feelings about their friend.

"Now, I have an announcement," said Eve, smiling. "You are all hereby invited for lunch at the opening of the Sunshine Flower restaurant this Saturday at noon. It should be a lovely event. So many changes have been made. You probably won't even recognize the place."

"That sounds like fun," replied Doty. "But, are you sure we're all invited?"

"Absolutely," responded Eve. "I got a call from Valerie, the new owner, and she said to be sure to invite some friends." Then, turning to Jackie, she continued. "Valerie also told me she's eager to meet you, so I hope you can join us, as well."

"I suppose so," said Jackie, cheerfully. "I think it's best to forget about the past and now, as you say, the restaurant has been re-done, so I won't be reminded of anything unpleasant. It's very nice of her to include me and I'm sure it will be lovely."

The next hour was filled with odd bits and pieces of superficial conversation. It seemed obvious to both Adam and Eve that everyone was trying their best to avoid discussing Jackie's recent incarceration and anything related to the murder. After they felt that they had spent an appropriate amount of time at Frank's reception, the Iversons excused themselves and returned home.

"That wasn't too bad," said Adam, as they entered their house. "I must say, Jackie certainly seems to be in good spirits, despite what she's gone through. She didn't show the least bit of resentment or anger."

"I think she was the only happy person there," replied Eve. "I'll bet we have another hung jury. Doty and Frank are probably willing to accept her self-defense story, but I'm not so sure about Paula. She hardly said a word and did you notice her expression? She never smiled, not even once."

"So, you still don't believe Jackie," sighed Adam.

"I just have some lingering doubts that won't go away . . . nothing based on any evidence, just my own personal gut feelings. I noticed she was wearing her favorite red dress and I suddenly remembered Little Red Riding Hood and the Big Bad Wolf. I wonder if

she had the same thought when she went to confront . . ,
or kill, her adversary. It may sound silly, but it was just
a flashing mental image. I've also been thinking about
something Doty said a while ago . . . on the day of the
barbecue. When she came over to our house, she told
me that Jackie's husband had died suddenly. She never
said how he died, just that it was sudden."

"You really are suspicious. I hope you're not going
anywhere with all of this nonsense," replied Adam,
curtly, as he tried to control his impatience. "It's over.
There's nothing more to think about."

"Believe me, I would like to let everything go,"
responded Eve, "but, I can't help where my thoughts
lead me. You might want to warn Frank to be a little
careful around Jackie. I also think you should be a little
wary, as well. Who knows? She may get another gun
and it certainly seems that the men in her life don't fare
too well."

"Let's just put an end to this nightmare. We have
some normal lives that we have to get back to. Try not
to forget why we moved here."

"You're so right," sighed Eve. "Even though I don't
think we'll ever know the real truth, I'll do my best to
put it all out of my mind."

Chapter 14

On Saturday morning, after a short ride on the new exercycle, Eve felt she needed to do something else to help stretch her muscles. Even though she was somewhat reluctant, she decided to go for a swim.

"I just love our new exercycle," she said to Adam, as she went back into the house, "but, I also enjoy doing laps in the pool, so I'm going to risk it."

"You're gonna turn into a real jock, if you don't watch out," replied Adam, teasingly.

"Don't be silly. I feel so good in both my mind and body, when I exercise. I think you could use a little more, yourself," chided Eve.

"As a matter of fact, I may do just that, while you're gone," retorted Adam.

Sure enough, when she arrived at the pool, Eve saw that it was surrounded by people who appeared to be deeply engrossed in animated conversation. She was about to turn and leave, when she heard Peggy Walsh calling her name.

"Eve, please don't go. Come here and sit by me. We'll find another chair," shouted Peggy. "We've all read the paper and I'm sure you already guessed what everyone is talking about."

Eve felt it would be rude to abruptly leave, so she walked over to her friend. Fortunately, she thought, there were no empty chairs.

"Here, take this one . . . I'm just leaving," announced a woman Eve didn't recognize.

There was little Eve could do to refuse, so she accepted the woman's offer and sat down. Sure enough, the news of Jackie Quinn's release had spread like wildfire throughout Sunshine Valley. A small crowd immediately began gathering around her, eager to hear what she had to say. One after another, they began shouting questions at her:

"What did Jackie have to say about being in jail?"

"Is she very upset?"

"Do you think it was self-defense?"

"Is she really free?"

"Is she allowed to leave the country?"

"Does she still have a gun?"

"Is she going to stay in Sunshine Valley?"

"I'm sorry, but I don't have anything to report," Eve stated firmly, as she looked around at the eager faces. "I only know what I read in the paper or hear on the news . . . same as everyone else."

"Is she coming to the pool today?" asked Peggy.

"I have no idea, but I tend to doubt it. She's been gone for quite a while, and I would imagine she needs to get her personal life in order, before she goes swimming again."

Eve was beginning to lose what little patience she still maintained. Without another word, she took off her robe and sandals, then jumped into the pool. After completing several laps, she finally felt herself beginning to relax. *I suppose I can't blame them,* she thought, philosophically. It's only natural for people to be curious, especially when murder is involved. She also had to admit that she too was curious. She wondered if most people believed the self-defense claim, or if they thought Jackie actually committed premeditated murder. But, she wasn't curious enough to engage in idle gossip.

When she felt she'd had enough exercise, she climbed out of the water, walked back to her chair, and began drying herself. "I wish I had something to tell you, but, I really don't know much," she announced to the group that had gathered around her.

As Eve prepared to leave, Peggy Walsh and the other onlookers remained silent, obviously disappointed that she wasn't willing to engage in conversation.

"Now, I have an appointment, so I'm afraid I can't stay here any longer." She pulled on her robe and sandals as quickly as possible, then turned and headed for the gate.

As she was leaving, she heard Peggy Walsh make another comment. "I also saw your picture in the paper...very nice. I'll be sure to go to the restaurant and see your painting."

"Have a fun swim?" asked Adam, when Eve returned home.

"The swim was fine. It's just all the people there who want to know about Jackie, and I'm not ready to talk about her."

"Was she there?"

"No, thank goodness, but, I'm afraid she's going to have a very difficult time when she does try to go swimming again. She'll be hounded with questions and, as she said, she doesn't like to talk about herself. I must say, I don't envy her right now."

Eve walked into the bedroom, took a quick shower, then dressed for the luncheon. "Well, I'm ready," she said, as she walked into the den. "Now, I'm finally going to have the chile rellenos and guacamole that I've been waiting so long for."

"We should probably be going," said Adam, as he pushed himself up from behind his desk. "Frank is taking his car and will pick up Doty, Paula, and Jackie. I told him to be at the restaurant at noon, but, it may be a little hectic inside. I'd like to get there before they arrive. So, if you're ready, let's go."

"Take care of the house," said Eve, as she leaned over and petted Coco on her curly head.

Within minutes, Adam and Eve were seated in their car. As they pulled out of the driveway, they noticed more people than usual walking along their street.

"This is very odd," sighed Eve. "I'll bet anything this increased foot traffic has to do with Jackie. I wonder what it'll be like at the restaurant. I hope it's not too chaotic and that people don't pounce on her. I'd like to have a nice, quiet lunch. I hope that's not asking too much."

Adam remained silent and kept driving.

"What a beautiful time of year this is," commented Eve, as she changed the subject. "I haven't had much chance to really appreciate all the plants that are now in bloom . . . so many lovely colors." She continued looking out the window, smiling. "I think we should go for a ride through the desert one day, before all the flowers wilt."

"We can do that. It helps us remember why we moved here," replied Adam.

When they arrived at the restaurant, Adam pulled into an empty space, close to the entrance. "Well, here we go again," he said in an ironic tone. "We've come full circle, but, I'm sure it'll be better, this time."

As they sat in the car, waiting for their friends to arrive, they noticed a sign in the restaurant window that read *Welcome Home, Jackie.*

"I was afraid of this," sighed Eve.

"Maybe it won't be too bad," replied Adam, in an attempt to calm his wife.

"Don't count on it," said Eve, curtly.

After a few minutes, they saw Frank pull up to the entrance, whereupon Doty and Paula emerged from the car.

"Let's go," said Adam.

"Where's Jackie?" asked Eve, as she and Adam walked over to their friends.

"I thought she'd be with you," offered Doty. "I called her this morning, but there was no answer. I thought she might be at the pool. When we drove to her house to pick her up, she wasn't home and the car was gone, as well."

When Frank joined them, he was also surprised not to see Jackie.

"Let's go inside," offered Adam. "She probably took her own car and will be here shortly. But, now, I think we'd better go in, before too many people start arriving. I know they're expecting us. We can wait for Jackie inside."

Adam and Eve led the way into the restaurant. Upon entering, the hostess greeted them with a smile.

"Good . . . you're here. We were waiting for you. I hope this visit will be more pleasant than the last time you were both here. Look," she said to Eve, "your picture is hanging up." She pointed to the framed newspaper article that hung on the wall next to her booth, then motioned to Maria, who immediately joined them. She was also smiling.

"Welcome back," chirped the woman, as she looked at Adam and Eve. "We have a nice table set up for you and your friends. Please follow me."

"We're expecting one other person," said Adam, "but, I think we can sit down. We'll look out for her."

Maria led the group to a table by a window that was set for six persons and included a beautiful vase of fresh flowers in the center.

"This is good," said Frank. "The view is perfect. We can watch and see when Jackie arrives."

"You should be very pleased. Your painting has received quite a few compliments," said Maria to Eve, as she pointed to the canvas on the back wall.

"It's beautiful," remarked Doty. "I've only seen the picture in the paper. Now, I get to see the real thing. I love it. You're a real inspiration, Eve." Both Paula and Frank nodded in agreement.

As everyone sat down, Eve took a seat that enabled her to clearly view her commissioned painting. It gave her a deep sense of pride to see it so prominently displayed. Although it was still early, most of the tables were occupied and she observed some diners pointing to her canvas and smiling. Occasionally, someone would wave to her and she would casually return the greeting. Looking around the room, she also noticed that her original stolen cactus painting was still hanging in its original place. *How ironic*, she thought. *If it hadn't been for that canvas, we wouldn't be sitting here now.*

It didn't take long before Valerie approached the group. "Where's Jackie? Didn't you invite her? I hope she'll be joining us." She sounded alarmed.

"Yes, of course, we invited her. She'll probably be coming any minute now," replied Eve, in an attempt to placate Valerie, even though she didn't believe her own words. She couldn't explain why, but she had an eerie feeling that, for some unknown reason, Jackie would not be making an appearance.

"Well, we're waiting. All the people who work here want to welcome her home and cheer her on. George Gomez even made a special cake for her. Meanwhile, I'm glad all of you were able to make it and I hope you enjoy your lunch. In the meantime, I'll have a waiter bring you some margaritas," she added hurriedly, then turned and went back into the kitchen.

"The dining room looks very different," remarked Adam, "much lighter and more modern."

"Yes," added Paula. "It also seems more cheerful."

"I think the redecoration is perfect and I'm glad you like it too," said Eve. "I've been here so many times since Valerie took over the restaurant. I forgot that none of you have seen all the changes that have been made. She's worked very hard to create a different look."

"Your painting fits in perfectly," added Adam.

Now and then, a server would approach the table to see if Jackie had arrived, but, to no avail. One waiter brought six margaritas and was puzzled to see that there were only five people seated at the table.

"You can put that last drink over there," said Frank, as he pointed to an empty place setting. "Our friend should be arriving shortly."

After reviewing the menu and finishing two bowls of chips and dip, Paula finally spoke up. "I don't think Jackie's going to come here today. Even though she said she'd be joining us, she probably thought her presence would draw too much attention. I'll bet anything that she's already there, or, on her way to Mexico to visit her cousins. I have a strong suspicion that she wanted to get as far away from Sunshine Valley as possible . . . at least until things quiet down."

"You may be right," chirped Doty. "I did hear her say she hadn't seen her cousins in years, but she didn't mention anything about going to visit them now. I can understand her desire to get away, but, if that's what she decided to do, I wish she would have told one of us. I wonder if she has a passport. I think you need one these days to travel to Mexico."

"Yes, she does have one," remarked Frank. "She told me it was confiscated when her house was searched, but she got it back when they released her."

"I think it's time for us to place our orders," said Adam. "We shouldn't have to wait much longer. Jackie can order if, and when, she arrives."

"Good idea," added Paula. "I'm hungry. Do you all know what you want?"

Everyone nodded and agreed that they were ready.

Adam motioned to a passing waiter, who came and took each person's order.

"Finally," sighed Eve. "Now, I get to have the chile rellenos I've waited so long for."

Once the food arrived, they all began eating. There was very little conversation and each person finished eating rather quickly.

"This was fabulous," remarked Eve. "It was worth waiting for. Did you all enjoy your food?" Each person nodded in agreement, but no one made a comment. Even though everyone drank their margaritas, the liquor didn't seem to have a positive effect on Jackie's friends.

"I know she can seem a bit erratic at times," said Eve, as she broke the silence, "but I can't believe that Jackie would just disappear without saying a word." Although Eve wasn't particularly looking forward to the chaos that Jackie's arrival would create, she began to feel some concern for the woman's safety. She recalled how George Gomez had almost been run down by some men in a car and wondered if they wanted to hurt Jackie as well, now that her crime had been made public.

"I spoke with Jackie last night," interjected Frank. "She sounded happy and said she was looking forward to having lunch with us. I thought I was getting to know her, but I guess I was wrong. I can't understand why she didn't show up, or why she didn't tell anyone she wasn't going to join us."

Although Adam had shared with his wife some of the misgivings Frank had expressed to him about Jackie, this was the first time Eve had heard him openly voice his negative feelings about the woman. Eve looked at Frank's sad face and thought he must be deeply disappointed.

"I hope she's okay," sighed Doty. "I hope she hasn't been arrested again." She looked around the table, but there was only silence.

After a few minutes, a waiter came and removed each person's plate. He was followed by George Gomez, who was holding a cake. "I baked this especially for Miss Quinn," he said. "I thought she'd be here."

As George placed the cake on the table, Eve spoke up. "We've been waiting for her, but she must have been detained. The cake looks lovely. Even though Jackie isn't here to enjoy it, we certainly will. We can take a piece with us and give it to her later. Do you think you could bring a bag?"

"I'll be right back," replied George.

Unfortunately, not one person at the table wanted any cake. When George returned with a large bag, Eve looked at him and smiled. "If it's okay with you, perhaps we'll just bring the entire cake with us. We can all share it at home, when we're together with Jackie. Thank you so much for all your effort."

Although George looked disappointed, he nodded, then placed the entire cake in the plastic bag.

After a few more moments of silence, Adam spoke up. "I think we can leave now. It doesn't look like Jackie will be joining us, after all."

Everyone nodded in agreement and raised themselves, then made their way to the exit. With some hesitation, Frank picked up the cake and carried it with him.

"I'll meet you outside," said Eve to the group. "I'm going into the kitchen. I want to find Valerie and Donna and thank them for the lovely meal."

After expressing her appreciation and apologizing for Jackie's absence, Eve returned to the dining room and eased her way through the crowded aisles to the front door.

When everyone was outside, Eve began to speak. "Why don't the three of you come over to our house. Even though Jackie isn't here to join us, I think we can do justice to this cake."

With a few sighs, the three friends looked over at Eve and acknowledged her offer.

When they got into their car and began driving towards home, Adam turned to his wife and spoke. "Well, Honorary Deputy Iverson," he said, with a smile. "What do you think? Are you ready to solve another mystery?"

Eve didn't say a word and simply glared at her husband. The only sound that could be heard on their trip home was a lone siren whistling somewhere in the desert.

Once again, as Adam and Eve pulled into their driveway, they heard Coco barking. Only, this time, she was on the patio. As they pushed open the gate, the couple was greeted by their dog, which quickly scampered between them and the exercycle. To their great surprise, there sat Jackie, peddling away.

"Jackie . . . you're here," exclaimed Eve, in astonishment.

Almost simultaneously, the back gate opened and in walked Doty, Paula, and Frank, who was holding the cake.

Doty rushed over to her friend and breathlessly began to speak. "Jackie . . . what are you doing here? Why weren't you at the restaurant? We were waiting for you and so many people wanted to meet you and welcome you home."

As she smiled broadly and looked around at everyone, Jackie stopped peddling. "I'm sorry. I hope I didn't keep you waiting too long. I had an early appointment with my hairdresser and thought I'd be finished in time. After all my weeks in jail, I felt I needed some work done on my hair and a manicure, before I could be seen in public again. But, as usual, I ran late. I tried calling you, Frank, but there was no answer . . . so, I left a message. I said I'd meet you at the restaurant. However, once I started driving there, I began to feel a bit uneasy. I wasn't too keen on having a lot of folks pounce on me and when I saw all the cars in the parking lot and the sign in the window with my name on it, I decided not to go in. I really hate being the center of attention. At one point this past week, I even thought about going to Mexico for a while to visit my cousins, but I don't fancy the long drive and I have no desire to leave my friends. I want to stay in Sunshine Valley and make a nice, quiet home for myself. So, I thought I'd just come back here and wait for all of you to return . . . even get in some exercise. I hope you understand."

"Yes, of course," replied Doty. "The main thing is that you're safe."

"We were afraid something might have happened to you, but we're so happy to see that you're okay," added Paula.

"What's with the cake?" chirped Jackie. "Is it somebody's birthday?"

"No," replied Frank. "George Gomez made this cake especially for you. Since you didn't come to the restaurant, we brought it home. Perhaps, now, we can all enjoy it together."

"How thoughtful," replied Jackie. "I'll have to call him later and express my appreciation."

Eve continued looking at Jackie and, even though she wasn't wearing her red dress, she thought she looked better than ever.

"I think we should all go inside and have some cake," announced Adam. "It's getting a little hot and it might be too uncomfortable out here on the patio. "Here, Frank," he added. "Let me take the cake. We can all go into the dining room."

As suggested, everyone, including Coco, followed Adam into the house.

"Please sit down. I'll make some coffee to go with our beautiful cake," said Eve, then turned and went into the kitchen, where she joined her husband.

"Looks like we're getting a bit back to normal," remarked Adam. "Everyone's mood certainly seems to have shifted. They all seem much more upbeat, compared to the restaurant. Even Paula had a smile on her face."

"I don't get it. Even though her behavior appears so erratic at times, Jackie certainly seems to have a viable explanation for everything she does. Perhaps she's okay and I'm the one who's a little nuts."

"Well," said a smiling Adam, as he put his arm around Eve, "remember . . . nobody's perfect."

THE END

ABOUT THE AUTHOR

 Rita Strombeck has a Ph.D. in Scandinavian Studies and an M.A. in French from the University of Chicago. Like her heroine, Eve Iverson, she taught languages for several years and enjoys painting. In 1982, she started her own business. Over the years, she has developed more than 50 education books and programs for health care professionals and the general public. Rita also received 12 grants from the National Institutes of Health (NIH) and has written successful grant proposals for various nonprofit organizations. She currently lives in Palm Springs, Florida, and wrote an article for *Palm Springs Life* magazine (March, 2013) on the city's early women entrepreneurs—"Women With Vision."

Rita has been a fan of mysteries since early childhood. In 1987, she participated in a small three-week workshop conducted by famous English mystery author P.D. James at the University of California, Irvine. Ms. James was very inspiring and encouraged Rita to continue writing. And so, she did. After completing her first cozy mystery with Cozy Cat Press, HOT TUB OF DEATH, she now has written her second cozy mystery—CORPSE IN THE CACTUS.

www.ingramcontent.com/pod-product-compliance
Lightning Source LLC
Chambersburg PA
CBHW020328260626
47156CB00004B/1431